# BUILT FOR PRESSURE

## TWINS LOVE STORY

## VINEE RAYNELL

D1557188

Built for Pressure
Copyright 2019 by Vinee Raynell

Published by Mz. Lady P Presents

All rights reserved

This book is a work of fiction. Names, characters, places, and incidents either are the product of the author's imagination or are used fictitiously and are not to be construed as real. Any resemblance to actual persons, living or dead, business establishments, events, or locales or, is entirely coincidental.

No portion of this book may be used or reproduced in any manner whatsoever without writer permission except in the case of brief quotations embodied in critical articles and reviews.

# SYNOPSIS

Lunya and Luna Wright are nineteen years young, identical twin sisters with different views. Their parents and older brother adore them both.

Lunya is the free-spirited twin, extremely smart and always down to blow smoke with her bestie. She has always clashed with her unapologetically black mother as long as she could remember. Living the college life, she is self-efficient with school and her side business. After an incident in high school, she is constantly getting curved by Marshad "Mars" Hudson, a long-term protégé of her older brother and cousin. She has always been attracted to him, yet he rejects her time and time again. When Lunya places that pressure, will he still be able to reject her?

Luna is the hard-working, selfless twin. Pregnant at fifteen from her first time having sex, her luck has always been a bit questionable. Though she adores her baby girl, Alani, she tries hard to work through the draining issues surrounded by her baby father. However, when the pieces don't fit, they don't fit. Crossing paths with the ambitious Kyrie Mikson, he wants what he wants and has no issue putting that pressure on her. Will the Wright twins' hearts shatter in pieces, or are they built for pressure?

# ACKNOWLEDGMENTS

"Always give thanks to your worth"
I want to acknowledge me for all this hard work
I want to acknowledge me for never quitting
I want to acknowledge me for trying to do more right then wrong
I want to acknowledge me for believing in me
I want to acknowledge the higher power
I want to acknowledge my parents for creating me
I want to acknowledge my publish for her support
I want to acknowledge my editor for improving my skills
I want to acknowledge all the people who see the universe in me
I want to acknowledge YOU for choosing this book
THANK YOU

#OutspokenVines #QueenLife #RoyalDreams

# SHATTERED DIAMONDS

Pressure creates warriors and diamonds!
When built for pressure you see beyond the agony.
Breaking is never an option.
Find sanctuary in my belief that the universe will always guide me.
Holding me close to her chest
I've created stars by just going hard and doing my part.
It's okay to be broken since I'm keeping it pushing
Even when people hurt me, break my spirit, and shatter my heart into millions of pieces.
Understand that I am built for all the doubt and pressure
So I don't mind anymore if those haters slander me.
I'm gone always win by staying true to myself
Knowing my worth
Even when I'm broken.
As a black queen, I make pain look like royalty
Of course, they shatter me
Everyone wants a part of me
I'm shattered diamonds!
Of course, I'm sparkling.
~Tha Vinee ~

# 1

## LUNYA "NYA" WRIGHT

Smoking my blunt, I looked over at my best bitch Kamoni. Rolling my eyes at her anti-social condition, I pulled my locs up and started shaking this ass. Looking at my brother mugging me, I smiled at him. Saved by Diamond, she distracted his uptight, annoying self. Thank God for sisters-in-law, yeah. My twin sister, Luna, had left early after the reveal of the new addition to the family! I gave Luca a black balloon with a huge white question mark on it. Inside contained a small glittery pink basketball that fell to the floor after he popped the balloon. Dime had a big black box with a white question mark as well, that held a glittery purple balloon that said "it's a girl" which floated to the ceiling as soon as she removed the gigantic lid of the box. Luca popped the balloon, while Dime lifted the lid. The rest of us held an identical hand sized black box as Dime's huge one. We all lifted our boxes, which contained a pink or purple cupcake with "it's a girl" in the frosting. I had put this together with Dime, and it was the best gender reveal ever.

I started thinking about my sister and the frustrated expression on her face as she rushed out of here after the gender reveal. She was out having a family night with her baby dad and, my pooh, Alani. I missed my baby anytime she wasn't around her Tete Mom. *She looks just like us, real shit.*

Plopping down on Moni's lap, I handed her the blunt. She was in her feelings about Cole's uglass. He had my girl fucked up. I'm going to mind my business though.

"He wanna play like I won't go over there and slap him and that hoe he entertaining."

"He knows you're trying to do better, Moni. Leave that man to his mess and be great!"

Jumping off her lap, I pulled her up. Shaking her ass, I hyped my bitch up. After a couple of shots, she was in her bliss. I bucked her up. I ain't want her thinking about Cole's foolery. My girl was in love with that nigga, yet Cole was too busy being a wild boy.

At twenty-one years old, he wasn't thinking about Kamoni and being with her long term. I wanted my girl happy, but that nigga stayed trying to get a reaction out of her. Moni was cool, calm, collected but she definitely wasn't pussy. She would snatch a bitch if pushed. I just didn't give a fuck enough to be pressed. At nineteen, I was living my best life. The only baby I needed was Lani. Good thing Luna had her for me. I'm so blessed to be a twin.

Taking another shot, I walked over to my brother and cousin. They were both in love, and I was here for it. Happy that I will be planning the baby shower for the incoming little queen, I hugged Diamond and rubbed her belly. I just loved her. Looking over at Rayna, I was so tickled at how mean that damn girl is. She definitely has a grip on that shit since she and my cousin made it official, but she was still Rae. She asked for my help with the baby shower since she had moved to Atlanta with my cousin. I love it.

Ready to feel greater, I bounced my ass to the kitchen to get another drink. Bumping into Mars, I was giddy as shit. He was always trying to play me out. For the universe in me, I couldn't fathom that shit. I licked my lips, looking up at him.

"Excuse you, sexy," I told him.

"Chill out," he said, moving around me, causing me to roll my eyes.

Continuing on my way, I grabbed another drink. As I turned around to head back in the party area, the drink was snatched out of my hand. Ready to go in on whoever did that shit, I opened my mouth but closed it instantly, realizing it was my mother. *Here she goes.* I love my mother, but she could be so annoying. I wasn't above letting her know how I felt when she's doing too much. I really didn't want any real smoke with Nubia though. I'll just tell my daddy if she gets to tripping too hard.

"Yo ass must want me to hurt you. Don't grab another fucking drink out my kitchen, Lunya Nuji Wright! I will beat yo ass in here!"

*See, just extra!* I was almost twenty, like bruh a drink ain't ever hurt nobody. Knowing she was close to blowing my high. I just walked out of the lady's kitchen. Rolling another blunt, I went outside. Seeing Mars, I went with my move on him again.

"Why you always trying to play me? Like I'm not ugly, and I'm not dumb. What's up with you?" I was tired of his shit.

"Look, ma. I'm twenty-two years old, and your brother is my dawg. I'm not feeling you like that Little, so just let it go." He's been calling me Little since the incident. Hitting my blunt, I stood in front of him.

"What's not to feel though, Mars? You're speaking on my brother, yet he's inside with his woman, and you're rejecting yours." I licked my lips.

"Lunya, back yo ass up son." Ignoring him, I stepped closer.

"I'm saying... Luca doesn't have anything to do with you and me." He pushed me back and chuckled.

"Your interest is cute. I really appreciate it ma, but I ain't feeling you, and there's a lot not to feel, baby." He looked me up and down as if he was unimpressed. Trying my best not to let him get under my skin, I had to save face.

"Fuck you, Marshad. It's another man's gain, baby. You KNOW how I'm coming, so it's coo." I smirked.

Putting out my blunt, I went inside. Not feeling festive anymore, I went to find Kamoni. Seeing her holding a conversation with my cousin Zeriah, I decided just to text her once I made it upstairs to my room. I was beat.

~

EARLY THE NEXT MORNING, I woke up and got my clothes together for class. Rushing in the bathroom, I did not know Marshad stayed here last night.

"Girl, get your ass out!" I stood staring at his beautiful dick. I was stuck in a big penis trance. The man is blessed! As he put his dick away, I walked all the way in and turned on the shower, not saying a word as he washed his hands.

"So, you just gone act like a nigga don't need privacy? You real fucked up with it."

"First of all, Marshad Leroy Hudson, this is MY house. Go to your home if you want privacy, and second, whenever you stop playing on my top, that's gone be all me," I said, stripping out of my clothes and getting in the shower.

He just left out. I was feeling some type of way last night. There is no way this nigga is not feeling me. He's just playing hard to get because of the incident.

After a quick fifteen-minute shower, I got ready for class. It was early as hell. Once I went downstairs, I smelled bomb ass food, and I needed parts of it! Luna has cooked breakfast. I was hungry as hell, so I was here for it. When Mars came into the kitchen, I made his plate. After eating, I had an hour before I had to be in class, so when Mars went downstairs in the chill room, I followed right on down behind him.

"Why you always acting like this?"

"Like what?"

"Like you don't want me," I said, getting all close on him. He moved me to the side, and I rubbed on his dick, he was hard.

"Move Nya, damn!"

I pulled his dick out and put my mouth on him. I gave him the sloppiest head ever. I was worried that I might choke and die as I tried to deep throat his dick. I licked the veins and slurped him up until he came. Swallowing his seeds, I got up to go upstairs. He looked drained and satisfied, which made me happy. He mugged the shit out of me as I left to brush my teeth and head off to class.

I WAS SITTING in my biology class honestly bored as shit. I was regretting the fuck out of not smoking before I came to this bitch. Anxious as hell to get out of class, I tapped my coffin-shaped nails on my desk as I patiently waited for my teacher to dismiss us. After finally getting dismissed, I left out heading to the library to link up with my homie, Kyrie. He was handsome, twenty-three, and about to graduate with a bachelor's degree in business. He was doing his thing.

He was fine, but we clicked on a friend level. He was my weed plug. I sold by the gram every now and again, nothing too major. I had a decent clientele, so I was making decent money. Plus Kyrie had that pressure! The weed sold itself. He had money, and I fucked with him the long way since he was somewhat family to my best friend, Moni.

His ambition to be more than a drug dealer was inspiring. He was a college student by day and the plug by night. I wasn't mad at him. We all got to eat some way out here, and I wasn't trying to punch anybody clock, so who the hell was I to judge the way this man make his money? I was a weed advocate. I honestly believe Mary Jane wasn't hurting anybody, and when annoying anti-weed people was all in my face on the bullshit, I suggested they ass give me and my blunt sixty feet. We weren't bothering anybody. I'm just trying to be happy and high.

"What you got going on later?" I asked Ky.

"Shit. I was gone pop out with the guys. There's a little event downtown. You should come through."

"For sure. I'll hit you up," I told him.

Grabbing the books I need, I headed on my way. I received a text from Luna, so I was getting my baby Alani today, which was cool with me. I was always excited about spending time with my pooh. Luna was working two jobs and taking online classes to be a registered nurse. I wanted her to pursue her dream and not settle for what she thinks she should do. Lani was always gone be straight. Amod wasn't a bad guy. In my opinion, he adored my niece, and she really didn't want for anything, but my sister didn't love his ass. She was settling! Luna was always trying to please someone, and I just wanted her to say "fuck everyone" including me and do something solely for herself. I knew she wouldn't, but I was working on sis!

I did some homework for a few hours to kill time before going by my parents' house where Luna and Lani are currently staying. I was taking Lani out to eat, and we were going back to my dorm to take a nap. I had a routine with my baby she is really accommodating to her Tete Mom, and I love that. I hope to have a daughter as sweet and smart as her one day.

Walking inside, I knew neither one of my parents were home. Going to the kitchen, I fixed me a snack. Eating the turkey sandwich and grabbing a bag of jalapeño chips, I went upstairs. Lani was on her mom's phone watching cartoons. Kissing her, I went into the bathroom to talk to Luna.

We looked exactly the same. There were only two ways to really tell us apart, one of which was our hair. Where I had locs, Luna had her natural curls going on. The second way was our body shape. I was slimmer with enough ass to make any man want me with small titties. Luna was thick. After she had Lani, her hips and ass sprouted. Her chest stayed pretty much the same, yet she had a hand full, and her shits were bigger than mine were. I watched as she stood in the mirror putting her hair in a bun.

"So, Amod will be picking up Lani from you in time for you to make it to your six o'clock class."

It was currently the summer semester. We were in July, so it was coming to an end soon, which I was extremely grateful for. I was taking biology, social work, and I had a late statistics class for six. Ready to go, I got Lani together, and we went to eat and back to my dorm and slept until Amod came to get her. Once my pooh was gone with her dad, I texted Kamoni about tonight.

**Me:** *Kyrie invited us out tonight.*

**Moni:** *I know. I'm with him now buying a half. He told me.*
**Me:** *Bet. Are you going?*
**Moni:** *Guhhhh maybe. Your cousin is stalking me. (Eye roll emoji)*
**Me:** *Oh my... (Laughing emoji)*

Getting ready for my statistics class, I dressed in blue jean ripped distressed shorts and a sheer black crop t-shirt top with a black block around the breast area with the word *Pressure* scrolled across it in red letters. I paired it with some white and red foam Jordan's. I had my locs half up on top of my head in a bun and the back hanging down my back. Getting a text, I had to make a sale before going to class. I grabbed the dub out of my stash that I had stored in my Tupperware bowl. Closing the lid, I placed the weed back in my drawer. I grabbed my book sack and headed to make this sale then off to class I went.

## 2

## LUNA WRIGHT

After a failed attempt of family night with Amod, I was drained. I love my daughter with all my heart. I truly do. Having her at fifteen was the scariest thing ever. I thought I was ready for sex until nine months later when I received this beautiful human. She was my world. Her father, on the other hand, was my damn headache. He had my parents' side eyeing me because he wrecked my car. He got it fixed, but he still talking about his mama got his, which I know is a lie, but I need Lani picked up from Nya in time.

It's an hour before my mother makes it home. So all I ask Amod is to pick her up and keep her for that hour, and that turned into him not having a car and needing to drive mine, like what the hell. I had the right mind to ask Luca. However, I didn't like having to rely on my family to help me with my parenting responsibilities. Amod could be more hands-on with Lani. She belongs to both of us. Pulling up at my parents' house, I parked, got out of the car and grabbed Alani out of the back seat. She had a lot of fun, and that warmed my heart if nothing else could. She passed out as soon as she got in the car for us to head home.

Grabbing my daughter and my belongings, I headed inside. My

mother and father are most likely asleep at three in the morning. My mother had probably put everyone out long ago. I was so happy about my baby niece coming into the world soon. Heading upstairs to my room, I sat everything down. I stripped my baby out of her clothes and put her nightgown on her. Then I placed her under the covers on her side of the queen size bed. Heading into the bathroom, I turned on the shower. Afterwards, I walked back into my room and grabbed my towel and clothes. Checking on Lani, she was knocked out, I mean snoring and every damn thing. I just smiled. Getting out my silk pajamas, I headed to the shower to wash the day off of me. After a very long well-needed shower, I dressed in my silk black pajama shorts and matching kami top, got in bed, and snuggled with my baby ready to get some rest.

Today I had the day off at both jobs, which was rare. Waking up to my baby, Lani was all in my face.

"I'm hungry. I need to eat eggs, cerea—"

"Alani," I stated, cutting her off. That was my child for real. Sitting up on my elbows, I responded.

"I'm gone feed you. You are going to eat. I got you. Eggs, bac—"

"Mama!" She giggled, giving me life with her pretty smile.

Pulling her in my arms, I hugged my baby tight. She changed my life. At fifteen years old, I didn't know shit about raising a baby. As I cried in my mother's arms about how against abortions I was, she allowed me to keep my daughter, and for that, I appreciated my mother for seriously considering me. If she had threatened to put me out or refused to help me, I would have had the abortion that Amod's parents desperately wanted me to have. I strongly felt I needed my parents at that time.

Getting out the bed, I slid into my house shoes and proceeded downstairs to the kitchen so that I could feed my kid. Deciding to make breakfast for the house, I whipped up French toast, breakfast potatoes, and turkey bacon. Satisfied with my cooking, I made Alani a plate and poured her some juice in her Princess Tiana cup. Handing her the Ruby Bridges book that we picked up at the library, she was all set for her morning routine. She reads her books while I skim through my Kindle looking for books to read. My daughter, at four years old, loves to read. It's adorable. She hounds me about going to the library when she finishes the five books that she gets during each visit.

"Good morning." My mother came into the kitchen and greeted Lani and me.

"Morning, maw-maw," Lani said, kissing my mother's cheek.

"Good morning, mom, what you got going on all dressed up this early?"

She had on some white dress pants and a peach short sleeve blouse. Her locs were in a bun showing off her face. My mother is breathtaking with her dark skin, high cheekbones, and full lips. Her locs reached past her waist. She's such a pretty lady. I'm a mama's girl where Lunya is not. I adore my mother.

"I'm going on a trip, getting a break."

Fixing her a plate, I handed it to her and asked about my dad.

"He is the one who put everything together. I don't know where we are going. As long as we are relaxing, I'm good." My mother loved trips.

"That smells good," Lunya said, coming to the island. Rolling my eyes, I started making her a plate.

"Good morning," I said to her hungry ass.

She usually stays at her dorm, so I wonder what made her stay here last night. Mars walked in immediately answering my question. Nya wanted his ass bad, but he refused to give my sister the time of day. Man, that shit is so funny. Being the thirst bucket that she could be, Nya washed her hands and made Mars a plate. I wanted to start cracking up, but I was gone let my sister be great. My mother said bye after I wrapped her plate to go. Making my own plate, I sat at the table to eat.

Scrolling my phone, I loved some pictures of Amod and Alani that he posted the other day. Amod and I were trying again, but he was continually cheating, which is why we stayed breaking up. I was tired of females telling me about being with him. I love Amod, but so much has changed, and I feel as if I may have outgrown him. I mean four years ago don't seem too long ago. However, I am a far away from the naïve fifteen-year-old that got pregnant by the class clown. Mod was getting older with me. He wasn't growing, and if he was, it was in the opposite direction.

I wanted Alani to have a two parent home like I did growing up. I was going to try with Amod, and we were going to work through the issues, yet I knew I was settling. He didn't give me butterflies anymore. As much as I wanted him to be the man for me for our daughter, I knew he wasn't. I just love the idea of him of being in love like the urban romance novels that I regularly read. Mod and I were constantly breaking up and getting back together. The entire back and forth was pissing me off. I desperately needed everything to work with Amod this time around.

Finishing my food, I cleaned the kitchen. My mother had left, and I was excited about my parents taking their upcoming trip. They deserved it.

"Mommy, I'm bored." Looking over at Lani, I was so tickled. At four years old, what does this baby know about being bored?

"Go read another book, Lani."

"Mama, I wanna go do something."

"Okay, baby girl, we can go do something." I kissed Lani's cheek. I really just wanted to chill today, but if my baby wanted to get out of the house, that's what we gone do.

I didn't know where Nya and Mars ducked off to. I wasn't too much worried about it though. The thing I hated most is that my sister felt like she had to beg that man to be with her. Nya was beautiful, smart, and free-spirited. She could have and deserved any man she wanted. Fuck Marshad if he couldn't see what he had in her. I admired my sister. She was a full-time student, and she didn't get pregnant at fifteen. I know my parents love Lani. They were still disappointed in me though.

I bathed Lani, showered, and got us dressed. I was ready to have a good day with my love bug. She looked adorable in the red overall dress she was wearing. She wore a short sleeve white undershirt on underneath. My baby has some coyly, long hair. I brushed it all up into a big puff. She wore white Chucks on her feet. I put in her diamond earrings that her "Sparkly" gave her on "their" birthday. Diamond loved her some Lani. I was so proud of my brother for finding a woman like her.

Dressing similar, I had on some red high waist biker shorts that hugged my hips and thighs perfectly. I put on a short sleeve white off the shoulder top and slipped on matching white Chucks. I took out the curling rods that I had put in my hair and separated my curls. I love my hair. I debated long and hard about twisting it into locs like my mother, sister, and brother, but I was just too attached to my big ass fro.

Looking at my phone, I had a text from my job. I had to go in for a little to help with coverage for a few hours. I didn't too much mind it. I love money. In the words of Cardi B, "*I got a baby I need some money.*" which is exactly right! I was still taking my love bug to do something, and then I was going to come back here and get dressed. Texting Nya, since I knew she was probably in her morning class, I asked her to keep Lani for me. Amod would pick her up for me because although these people said a few hours, that shit is really not for sure.

All dressed up, I picked Lani up and headed to my candy apple red Nissan Altima. Nya had a matching one, but hers was a champagne color. She has been begging our daddy to get her a Lexus since her shit kept breaking down. My parents were well off. I don't know too much about their background, but the foundation they built had me and my sister spoiled as hell. Luca not too much since he was born during the struggle. Apparently, my mama was an unapologetically, black, wild woman and did some wild shit that they didn't want us to know about. My mother was so full of love, but please do not piss her off she will cuss you out and lay hands and feet on you if necessary. She owns and works at a natural hair beauty shop. I stay dropping in there getting my hair washed for free.

Pulling up at the movie theater, we were going to see *Aladdin*. We had snacks in my purse. Getting out of the car, we went inside. I paid for the tickets, and we headed towards the theater room. A pretty little girl came running up to my baby. She was a light brown complexion with a messy bun on top of her head. She had on a cute little skirt and short sleeve hoodie jumpsuit on that just so happened to be red as well, matching Lani and my swag.

"Mommy, this is my friend, Jahanna."

"Jahanna!" a fine ass man called out. He had locs and tattoos. *Damn.*

He walked up mugging the pretty little girl, and he was not happy. I assumed little Jahanna was his baby. She definitely resembled him. She hid behind my legs as if I could save her from her daddy.

"Baby Jah, I will take your butt back home if you don't stop playing with me. What you got going on running off like that? He was frowning at her. As if he just noticed Lani and me, he smiled at me.

"Uncle Ky, I was saying hi to my friend, Lani," she said with glossy eyes.

Bringing his attention back to Jahanna, he picked her up.

"That's fine love, but you cannot just be running off like that. It's not cool at all Baby Jah."

"I sorry," she said in her small, cute voice.

"I'm Kyrie. You must be Luna. How you doing, love?"

"How do you know me?" I said, grabbing my baby hand and started towards theater eight where our movie was playing.

Following behind me, he chuckled. He told me he went to school with Nya and had seen me around a few times. He said he knew Nya had a twin, and he had just seen her on campus not too long ago. We picked the seats in the middle row; the girls wanted to sit together. We allowed the girls to sit next to one another. I was sitting by the girls, and Kyrie was sitting next to me. Baby Jahanna forgot all about her uncle as she sat chatting with Lani. They shared the small can of popcorn of caramel, cheddar, and white popcorn that I had snuck in here. Kyrie smelled good as shit. He kept looking at me. Every single time I felt his eyes on me, I felt like I would faint. I was attracted to his ass, yet I knew I was trying with Amod and didn't need to be having the fantasies that I was currently having about this man. I definitely need to focus on rebuilding my family.

After the movie, the girls were having so much fun together that we decided to take them to the park. I had a couple more hours to spare before Nya would be at my parents' house to pick up Lani so that I can head to work.

"Ms. Luna, can you get on the tire swing with us? My uncle is gone push us." Laughing at her demand, I told her to ask her uncle's permission first. She was adorable, and I could tell that Lani and her meshed well together.

Kyrie agreed to push us, so I got on the swing with the girls and allowed him to push us. I was thrilled that my baby was giggling having a good time. Alani Nubia Wright was my heart, and her smile meant everything to me. I never knew that I could love someone so much. I couldn't imagine life without my baby. Finishing on the swing, Kyrie played around with the girls chasing them around and catching them at the end of the slide. It was so adorable that I kept snapping pictures of them on my phone. I posted a few on my Snap, not thinking anything of it.

When it was time to part ways, the girls were so sad that I exchanged number with Ky so that Jah and Lani can have a play date soon. That seemed to cheer the girls up. Separating from Kyrie, I just couldn't stop thinking about him as I drove to the house. Pulling up at my parents' house, I parked and got out and unbuckled Lani. I headed inside the house, going straight upstairs with my love bug. I turned on *Lilo and Stitch*. I had my baby familiar with all the throw-back cartoons. I had the entire series of *Proud Family* and *Rugrats*. My baby was going to be exposed to all the 90s shows that I adored as a child.

Heading in the bathroom, once Lani was settled, I stripped out of my clothes and put on my scrubs. Nya came in soon after, and I confirmed with her that Lani would be picked up before her six o'clock class. Kissing my sister's cheek, I was so appreciative. She loved Lani so much and helped me out a ton that I would definitely consider her Lani's godmother. Alani was certainly her daughter too.

When I was up all those nights as a teenage mother, so was she! Amod was being so scary when Lani first arrived that Lunya was like the second parent to my daughter.

Hugging up on my baby, I kissed her bye and told her to have fun with her Tete Mom. Finishing up getting dressed, I left out and hopped in my car. I had let Amod know that he could not drive my car today. He needed to find his own way to get his daughter. I was so sick of Amod. He was a good father to Lani, and I knew he loved our daughter, but it was like he expected me to pull both of our weight. I was not with that shit. My baby girl was good regardless, but I wasn't gone keep allowing this nigga to slack. I have allowed him to be entirely too comfortable, and I needed him to understand that I was done with all his bullshit. There will be no getting back together if he cheats again. Hell, there will be no relationship at all but a co-parenting one, if he keeps playing on my top. The last few weeks after he got the car fixed, he has been dropping me off and picking me up so that he can get Lani. My only issue with this arrangement is that he drops Alani off with my mother right away as if he can't spend more time with her, and not only that, this nigga was joy riding in my fucking car when the only reason he has it at all is due to his daughter. I wasn't gone keep playing games with Mod about shit. It was a little hard being a young parent, but shit, his ass wasn't even doing the hard shit.

Pulling up at work, I received a text from Nya.

**My Face:** *Come out tonight, baby.*

**Me:** *No.*

**My Face:** *PLEASE!*

**Me:** *NO!*

**My Face:** *Why the hell not, Luna Nubi Wright?*

**Me:** *I'm not in the mood Lunya Nuji Wright.*

**My Face:** *Mom said she would watch Lani. Come on, LULU. Come out with me. Be fun damn!*

**Me:** *Byee Nya, I'll think about it.*

**My Face:** *Okayyy!*

Pulling up at the hospital, I worked as an assistant nurse. I parked my car, got out, and headed inside. I couldn't wait to be a registered nurse.

I SAT in the front covering the front desk and scheduling appointments. I had been here for a little over five hours, and I was ready to get the fuck out of here. I had been working all day, Alani was with my mom, and I felt good I could go out and have a good time. I was driving to Kamoni's house. Her older sister Kamora was going to do our hair and makeup before she headed back to Baton Rouge. Lunya told me to go straight there. She had my clothes, and she knew if I went home, I probably would have ended up cuddling with my baby and falling asleep.

I pulled up at Moni house and got out. Once inside, I went to the kitchen where Kamora was doing Moni's makeup. Lunya was fully dressed. She had on a black skirt with slits on the side, and a sheer red and black top. She paired it with red peeped toe booties. Her locs were beautifully styled in a huge bun on top of her head, and she had gold accessories matching the clips in her hair. She was next to get her makeup done. She gave me my bag of clothes, and I went upstairs to shower and get dressed. After a twenty-five minute shower, I dried off and wrapped the towel around me. I pulled out the sexy, royal blue mid-thigh dress. The back was out, and there was a decent amount of cleavage adding sex appeal. Silver blue heels and a diamond choker were in the bag.

After getting dressed and brushing my teeth, I headed back downstairs. Nya's face was done, and her lashes were bomb. Kamoni had long bundles in her hair that Mora had just finished wand curling. She went to get dressed while I got my hair and makeup done. We decided on a cute chain braid ponytail with a long, body-wave Brazilian bundle. It was cute and matched the dark lip and Smokey eye. Kamora was heading out she had to drop her friend off at the airport or something like that. Taking shots with my sister, I was good and lit.

When Moni finally came down, she was dressed in white high waist dress shorts and a lace pink off the shoulder top. She paired them with Gucci pink heels on her feet. We were all ready to head to the club. We piled into the Uber since everyone wanted to get drunk. I received a FaceTime call from Alani while we rode to the club. She appeared on the screen in her pink pajamas and bunny slippers. Sitting next to my mom with her legs crossed, they both had on their bonnets.

"Mommy, you look pretty, but where you at?"

"I'm out with Auntie Nya and Moni."

"I miss you," I swear I wanted to go home to my kid hearing her say that.

"I miss you too, daughter. What are you doing?"

"Maw-maw and me are just watching movies waiting on paw to get here with our snacks," she said.

"It's maw-maw and I Lani, and yawl gone have fun, yeah?"

"Yeah, mama. I love you. Have fun. Paw-paw just came in!" she excitedly said as she hopped up on the bed. We were pulling up at the club.

"I love you, love bug!" I said.

"Love you too, mommy," she said, ending the call.

We all hopped out, paid, and received our wristbands. The music was hot. I followed Lunya and Moni up to VIP. They greeted many people that I assume they know from campus. I had about three shots before Kyrie, the sexy dude from earlier, walked up hugging Nya and Moni. He briefly stared at me, causing me to bite my lip. He was fine as hell in a black short sleeve button-up, black jeans, and white Nike's. Damn, his locs were in a ponytail to the back, showcasing his sexy face.

"Hey gorgeous," he said in his smooth voice, instantly turning me on.

"Hey," I said, turning away and asking for another drink.

I was a ball of nerves and couldn't focus on anything but this man's cologne. He smelled sooo good. I took the shot. Nya spotted Mars and Cole.

"We will be right back, twin," she said.

I swear she better not start anything with that man after she damn near begged for me to come out with her. I wasn't for no mess right now! I was still facing the bar when I felt Kyrie ease behind me. He whispered in my ear.

"Calm down, baby. I'm not gone do you nothing," he said, planting a soft kiss on the side of my neck.

My heart was beating fast as hell. I was wet, and all those drinks were sneaking up on me. I was on my level. I felt anxious with Kyrie standing so close. Ky pulled me to the dance floor, and I started shaking ass, throwing my big booty all on him. I was having a bomb ass time!

# 3

## MARSHAD "MARS" HUDSON

Lunya and Kamoni walked up. Cole had a bitch in his lap, and I was chilling rolling this blunt. I didn't expect for Nya to suck my dick this morning. I was pissed for even allowing her little ass to even do that knowing it was gone cause issues. I was trying to avoid that altogether. Luca already had let me know that Lunya told him about *us*, but I had no fucking clue what he was talking about. Lunya is fine as hell, but she immature. I don't have time for little ass girls. A nigga is not R. Kelly! I'm playing. She is not that much younger than me, but her ass is spoiled as hell. She thinks she can do and have whatever and whoever she wants.

For example, this morning, I told her hardheaded ass to go on, and she whips out my dick blessing me with the best head a nigga done had in a long while just the way I taught her. I'm talking top-notch, sloppy toppy. A nigga was relaxed as fuck afterwards.

My ole lady walked up and kissed me. I made eye contact with Nya. Her ass had better walk away, or a nigga was definitely gone hurt her feelings. She smirked.

"Cole, you're pissing me off. You're so fucking disrespectful!" Kamoni said, knocking the bitch sitting on that nigga's lap clean off him and onto the floor. Ana hopped up, and I side eyed her ass. That shit was between them.

"Mars, that's my friend, and that bitch being extra," Ana said, knowing damn well she just wants to be involved in bullshit.

"Mind your business. That shit has nothing to do with you, love," I said simply.

"But that's—"

I hopped my ass up, cutting Ana off to grab Nya, who had just busted a bottle over Cole's head after he slapped the shit out of Kamoni. Josleen, Ana's friend that Kamoni pushed off Cole, ran up on Nya. I didn't have time for this dumb shit, so I pulled out my piece and aimed at the bitch, she stopped looking scared.

"Why are you pulling out on my girl and protecting that bitch, Mars?" Ana screamed. Nya was huffing and puffing mugging the fuck out of Kamoni who disappeared after Cole as he stormed out pissed.

"Let me go! I'm good."

"What the fuck yawl got going on?" Zeriah said, coming into our section.

"Not shit," Nya said, moving away from me.

Ana was staring hard as hell at that nigga Riah. I was staring at her ass like she was as dumb as she looked by being all in that nigga's face. I put my piece up. Nya seemed to be all in her head, and Ana was doing a whole lot. I gave her my *chill the fuck out* look, and right on time, a pretty, light brown, thick female came through. She had on blue jeans and a Saints muscle shirt. Her hair was in braids to the back, showcasing her face. She was definitely kin to Kamoni.

"Nya, where her stupid ass at?" she demanded, looking around.

"She ran off after dude ass," Lunya said, looking at Ana and shaking her head. Ana looked pissed, and for whatever reason, she was mugging the fuck out of Lunya.

"That shit is getting out of control, Kamora. Moni is fucking up," Nya said, looking sad and shit.

Since this situation wasn't my business, I was ready to get the fuck. Lunya was ignoring Ana, but I know how my girl is. She is gone force shit until Nya says something to her ass. She lived for the bullshit. Most days I think her ass thought she was on *Love & Hip Hop* with all that messy shit she be on. I didn't have time for the bullshit, but clearly, the universe didn't give a fuck that I wasn't in the mood.

"I'm about to chill at her house until she gets there thanks for calling me, Nya baby," the woman said as she hugged Nya and walked off. Lunya made eye contact with me.

"Bitch, move around all in my nigga's face. You so pressed to be like me."

"Ana, chill the fuck out son," I told her.

"Damn, I still got you feeling some way, guhh? Did I not give your baby daddy back to you? Why are you still worried about Nya? But I'm pressed? Bitch, beat it! Your nigga is about to be MY nigga, so don't worry about me being in his face!" Lunya stated like that shit was facts. She was talking real sporty, and I'll be capping if I said that shit didn't turn a nigga on, but since the bullshit that she pulled back in high school, I wasn't fucking with her childish ass. Ana ran up trying to attack Nya, but she wasn't ready for the tase that Nya gave her ass. I was shaking my head as I picked my girl up. I mugged Nya, annoyed that she brought her ass over to my section to begin with.

"Your ass is real fucked up with it, Little. A nigga is not fucking with you like that. You need to chill your ass out, you always sweating a nigga. Why the fuck did you tase my bitch?" I said pissed off.

Nya looked sad briefly until a pissed off expression took over her face.

"Fuck you mean why BITCH? You see why. Nigga fuck you, how about that!" She then stormed out of my section.

I wanted to go after her ass, but I knew Ana was in pain. A nigga is tired of dealing with bullshit.

After making sure Ana was good, I headed to see Luca. Luca took me under his wing when my brother got jammed up. I was out here in these streets by myself being a reckless ass nigga stressing my moms out. I was just a little nigga when I started helping them. My brother Shamar, also known by Riot, was in the streets heavy. Our father died when I was seven, and Riot was ten. Once Riot got out of jail, he moved back to Chicago with my mother where we are originally from.

Our dad located down to New Orleans. My mother loved Chicago, yet she was in love with my pops, Let her tell it, she would follow him anywhere. My mother had been down with my pops for a century. He was in the Army, and he later became a pilot. When he died from a blood vessel busting in his brain, my mother was heartbroken. Till this day, we don't know what caused that shit.

I fucked with Cole the long way. He has been my boy for a while now. I met the nigga in high school. I also fucked with Zeriah. I spent many days out in Atlanta getting rid of problems ordered by his brother Bear and cousin Luca. I stay clear of that nigga Bear nowadays. He's still fucked up about that Wilder situation and his shorty Rayna. I fucked up, and Bear fucked me up! He beat my ass good. I had some fractures and shit. I gave a good fight though. I wouldn't stand for no nigga beating my ass easily. I am nowhere near pussy.

I knew that man was in his right. I fucked up, and it almost caused his ole lady her life. Hell, a nigga is glad shit worked out because I wasn't gone fight that swole, muscle head nigga again. Fuck the dumb shit. I'll shoot Bear's big ass first! All jokes aside, I'm man enough to admit that I played a part in that shit that happened with Rayna. It was my fault for not keeping it real from the jump. Huss was my dawg, rest in peace to that nigga. I didn't think shit of it when his brother Wilder came instead of him the night Clout's place got raided, and Rayna got bumped. I knew I fucked up when the nigga whereabouts couldn't be found. That nigga Bear had my ass stressing out looking for that nigga.

PULLING up at a big ass mansion that Luca copped for Dime, I parked my Benz and got out. As I knocked on the door, it flew open. Diamond was out of breath. She was wide as hell with her swollen stomach. She frowned at me and slammed the door in my fucking face! That shit was rude and not even like her, but Luca said her ass could be mean as hell sometimes.

Opening the door, Luca apologized.

"You can relate to that foul ass nigga, huh? Yawl in the same boat with that sneaky fuck boy bullshit!" Dime said, fussing as she started walking upstairs where Nya stood.

Lunya rolled her eyes hard as hell at me as she and Dime disappeared in a room and slammed the door. *Well damn, a nigga didn't even do shit.* I followed Luca to his man cave as I started rolling a blunt to get my mind right. I was feeling the way they had this crib set up. The shit was DUMB! I know he had spent major bread for this place.

"Don't mind Dime ass, my guy. My daughter got her spazzing about any and everything, not to mention that bitch Hazel keeps calling my phone making excuses to get around me. Last week Dime's ass popped up at the restaurant to surprise me, and Ajinne had Hazel in that bitch! Shit went left. Dime's ass was about to fuck some shit up. Hazel is doing too fucking much. A nigga has been patient off the strength of our past relationship, and I do want to help her. Dime is tired of hearing that good nigga shit. Hazel is gone fuck around and have to go if she keeps playing these games with my wife. I'm trying to help her ass, but she is being hella messy.

Diamond is moody as fuck, one minute she's crying, and the next she making my plate and not bringing a nigga a utensil! She is walking her ass around saying smart shit about me helping Hazel. She is out of fucking control with the tears. Then your ass pissed Nya off. I already told her ass, whatever the fuck yawl got going on is between yawl. I don't want any parts in that shit. I got my own bullshit that I'm working out. Then on top of that, I can't tell my lady shit when it comes to the twins."

He was looking on his phone as he continued to speak.

"Dime is pissing me off with her constant mood swings. That's my baby though, not to mention she's been helping with the restaurants and even goes to Baton Rouge to help manage The Lounge. Wifey is pissed about that static she had with Hazel. Anything will set her ass off, especially with Hazel getting out of control with her bullshit.

Fuck, let me send these flowers. Yo boy is in the dog house," he said sparking up a blunt while picking out a vase of rainbow looking roses that he showed me on his big ass iPhone 8 Plus.

I just shrugged. I needed to clear shit up. I wasn't dogging his sister, nor was I trying to be with her ass. I'm pissed as fuck she tased my girl! Whether she is with the bullshit or not, I am not Nya's man. I'm good with my girl! I was praying this nigga could talk some sense into her, but as soon as I started talking that nigga cut me off.

"Nigga, I just told you I don't want no parts in that shit. The next thing you know my wife is pissed at me about YOUR shit! Nah my guy, figure your shit out. Just don't lay hands on my sister. Mane, she probably fucks with the pink ones. Nah, the rainbow roses go dumb," he said focused on the flower purchase he was trying to order to get back in good with Dime. I shook my head.

"Whipped ass nigga, I'm out."

"I whip the pussy too, my nigga. Fuck you," he said, not even looking up from what the hell he was doing.

I just chuckled. That shit too funny how in love the nigga is. He would do anything for that damn girl, and it was obvious.

As I walked upstairs to head out to my car, Nya was leaving out. Diamond was mugging the shit out of me as I bypassed her. I didn't too much give a fuck. I ain't do shit to nobody!

I'm a firm believer that I am not responsible for anyone else's feelings and won't say fuck mine to make another muthafucka feel good. I wasn't no grimy ass nigga on no type of level. I took accountability for my fuck ups always. Nobody had a reason to be on no fuck shit unless I do some foul shit, which I have not. A nigga just be chilling and trying to stay out the fucking way. My past was bleeding over into my present, and the shit was conjuring up old ass feelings that were supposed to be dead a while ago. It's crazy that the bitch Ana hated was Lunya.

She told me about the conflict over her baby dad. Ana had two kids. She was twenty-eight years old. Apparently, her baby dad was a dead beat. She told me about the little "young bitch" he was tricking on. She was heartbroken when I met her, bitter as hell, and stayed crying about that fuck nigga disrespecting her with a "toddler bitch" until a real man like myself came along making her pussy wet instead of her eyes! I was that nigga. I keep shit real with everybody. Check my damn credentials. I'd been ten toes down for a while now, and I wasn't the attention seeking type like some of these bitch ass niggas. I always stay clear of stupid shit. If I fucked up, I'm man enough to admit that shit.

I loved my girl Ana. She's been my bitch for about two years now. She had pretty bright skin. She was mixed with black and Asian, and she is beautiful. She had a curvy ass body that I enjoyed. The only issues I had with my baby is that she stayed accusing my ass of bull-shit. She was one of those women who tried to make the next man pay for another nigga's mistakes. I hated that shit and constantly had to tell her ass that I ain't that nigga. I wasn't perfect by far, but I love my girl. I just had some old feelings and shit for a fine ass female from my past that low key crushed a nigga with the shit she pulled back in high school. Then on top of that, another thing that prevented Ana and me from marriage is the way she carries herself. She acts a fool no matter where we are, and that shit is unattractive.

I walked out and snatched Lunya door open. She looked at me pissed off.

"Follow me."

"Nah, I'm good," she said hard but smooth as hell while pulling on the door to close it.

I wasn't letting up though. We needed to talk. All this back and forth shit was for the birds. Her tasing my girl was out of fucking line, and we both know she only did shit like that because she knew her wild ass could get away with it. Now that a nigga had to get her crazy ass together, her feelings were hurt. She fucked our shit up. Yeah, she was my Little until she started playing hoe games, one thing that I wouldn't put up with when it came to my relationship. A nigga's way too dope to be fucking with a bitch who wanted to hoe. Long story short, Nya could play that innocent fucking role all her sexy, petty ass wanted to. We both knew her ass shouldn't have brought her ass to my section to begin with.

"Aiight," she said, and I let her door go.

I had to rush to my whip and hop in since she immediately pulled off once I let her door go. I followed her ass across town some damn where. She parked and jumped out of her car. I continued to follow behind her until the girl she referred to as Kamora opened the door looking pissed.

I followed my ass inside after Lunya. Kamoni was on the couch pissed off, and hell, I was ready to leave at this point. This was too many hostile fucking vibes for your boy!

"Yo ass is real fucked up with it Lunya! How the fuck you gone call Mora about my fucking business *and* pull up with this clown ass nigga?" Kamoni spat with anger. Her whole body was shaking in rage.

Nya looked at me as if she just realized that I had followed her. Moni tried to walk up on Lunya, but her sister, I'm assuming, pushed her down on the cream-colored sectional.

"Don't play with me, Monkey! I'll beat your ass in here. YOU are pissed at yourself, not Nya. Your stupid ass is chasing behind that nigga looking like a goofy, breaking widows and shit. Yeah my girl, your ass is out of line! You need to be thanking HER! Fucking with me, your ass would have sat in the parish jail if it wasn't FOR HER!" Kamora yelled, looking like she would really beat that ass.

This wasn't my business, so I took my ass outside to wait on Lunya. I needed to talk to her ass before I called it a night. Hopping in my whip, I made myself comfortable as I texted my girl waiting on Nya to bring her ass out.

# 4

## LUNYA

After everything went down at the club and Moni went chasing after that bitch nigga, I was hurt as hell. That nigga just slapped her ass like she was living on the fucking stroll in front of a club full of people, yet this ditzy hoe is running after that nigga? Fucking right, I called Mora! The shit was no different from her calling Luca my senior year of high school. I got jammed up in some bullshit with Ana and her baby dad Skype, which is why that bitch Ana doesn't like me. Kamoni was doing the most pressing Cole's no good dog ass. I was just trying to look out for my best friend, yet my hands were tied, and I need assistance because my heart is in the right place, and the bitch wasn't listening to me.

Soon after I left the club, I got a call from an inmate, and it was Kamoni's stupid ass. I told Mora, and she refused to go pick her up. Talking about *"let her dick dizzy ass sit there."* Kamora was the big sister I always wanted growing up. Since I'd been Moni best friend, Kamora has always had my back! She was only twenty-three, yet the way she got it out the mud for herself and siblings was admirable as fuck. The bomb ass one bedroom Moni got, her sister pays for it. The bomb ass Lexus she pushes is all Mora too. They only have one living relative they know of to my knowledge, which is the beauty who raised them, their grandma Sugar Momma who I adored!

I bailed Moni out, dropped her ass off, not saying shit to her, and went straight to my brother's house. I was happy that Luna was finally having fun. She decided to stay and get a ride from Kyrie. I was pissed about everything, both Kamoni's and Marshad's bullshit. I loved him and honestly believed that I always will, yet he stayed trying to play me stupid!

Pulling up at my brother's house, I parked and used my key to get into the beautiful ass mansion. This bitch was DUMB! On my way here, I started thinking about my complicated shit with Mars. I had already told Dime that I was coming. She stood at the top of the stairs in a sports bra and yoga pants. Her tummy was poking out, and she looked like she would drop my baby niece at any moment! *She was big as hell.*

I met her upstairs and began telling all the shit that went on tonight. I even let her in on the history behind Marshad and I that only one person outside of us knew the real on. After about an hour of me running my mouth and crying nonstop about how Marshad's fake ass handled me at the club tonight, she finally gave me her input as she handed me some tissue to wipe my face.

"That man is playing games. He got you fucked up!" she said after telling her everything that went down not too long ago with Mars and Kamoni.

The frustration of being in love with a fronting ass nigga caused tears to pour down my face freely. I also couldn't believe how stupid Moni was out here acting.

"Don't cry, Nya! It's okay, pooh." Dime reached over hugging me.

We heard banging on the door, so she got up to get it. She was wobbling and shit. The struggle was real with my baby niece! I cracked a small smile, just thinking about the day Alani was born and how scared my sister was. My mind was on that magical and scary ass moment when I heard Dime talking shit to Luca. I wondered if Hazel had done some more fuck shit, so my nosy ass went to check who was at the door. Seeing Marshad instantly had me rolling my eyes and heading back in the room. *Stupid ass nigga.*

After returning to the guest room with Dime, we talked about her wanting to beat Hazel ass. As we joked and I started feeling better about the situation with Mars, I got a text from Kamoni, and she was pissed off. I decided that I was gone pull up, fuck all the text arguing back and forth shit. If she wanted to come for me, she was gone do that shit in my face. I've been nothing short of a solid and caring ass best friend to her ditsy ass. She was talking a lot of bullshit via text message right now, and I wasn't having it.

Leaving out the house, I walked right pass Mars like his ass didn't exist and hopped in my car. Starting it up, my door was snatched open by Marshad. *He is giving me a migraine! Damn.* Desperately wanting to get away from him and his mind games, I agreed to follow him so that he can let my door go. As soon as he did, I sped off to Moni's shit looking in my rearview. He was following me at first, but I didn't see him anymore once I hit the interstate. Thinking I lost him, I proceeded to Moni's crib. Once I arrived, my focus was solely getting to the bottom of the bullshit that she was sending to my phone.

Knocking on the door, Kamora allowed me in. She was saying something, but my attention was on my best friend. Her face that was drenched in tears as she bounced her leg in annoyance. Moni was upset.

I was surprised when she pinned me with a mug, yelling, "Your ass is real fucked up with it, Lunya! How the fuck you gone call Mora about my fucking business *and* pull up with this clown ass nigga?"

Looking behind me, it was definitely a clown ass nigga staring back at me—*fuck Mars!*

Moni tried to walk up on me, but Kamora blocked her. Marshad had left out soon after Mora snapped on Kamoni. His ass should have gone by his bitch instead of stalking me anyway. Moni was mugging me. Today was just a fuck me day! My feelings were hurt by the way she was currently acting. I still felt some type of way on how she ran after that nigga begging him to talk to her. This girl staring at me with hatred wasn't my best friend. This bitch was embarrassing.

I sat my ass down to roll a blunt. This entire situation had my nerves bad. I will call Mora every time if my friend is self-destructing. I don't give a fuck, especially if I can't do shit about it. Cole is a garbage ass nigga, and he likes the play woman beater games with my friend! Fuck minding my business. My friend needs help. Moni is honestly mad because Kamora is the true definition of "my sister's keeper." She doesn't give a fuck, and she always makes time to check Moni when she is fucking up. I wasn't excluded from that shit either! She is tough love in a sexy ass woman form. She is definitely the pressure queen.

"I hate you, Mora! Fuck you, Nya. That's why Mars dogs the shit out of you! You all in my business judging me like you haven't let that nigga drag you. How dare you sit in my face and rat to Kamora like you're not a pressed bitch? Buddy's ass is not even your nigga!"

I laughed, but there wasn't shit funny. I dead ass wanted to flash out, but I wouldn't make it easy for her to blame me for her fucked up situation. I was a lot of shit and I had a lot going on when it came to Marshad Leroy Hudson. He had my heart, and I was working my ass off after tonight to reclaim my shit. She didn't know much about what he and I had going on. Moni's ass was reaching, and seriously stupid as fuck trying to label *me* a pressed bitch when we *both* knew, she definitely owned that damn title with her stupid ass! Pressed? Nya? Bitch bye! I lit my blunt, inhaling.

"Do you really think that we can take your ass serious right now? I hate to be the one to tell you, shawty. Don't nobody give a fuck about that fake ass anger, my girl! *You* are the problem. Monk, is this the type of woman you want to be? Let me get some life insurance money if you gone act like a weak hoe. All in the club letting this nigga put his hands on you! Acting ridiculous? Sitting your stupid ass in the parish to get out and suck the nigga's dick who out here disrespecting you? Make it make sense, or I'm fucking you up!" Mora spat. She was big mad.

Kamoni was crying hard as hell, and no flex, I felt bad for my friend. She is hurting. She loves Cole. I mean she seriously loves that man. I knew all too well how painful it was to love a nigga who was no good for you. Even though I did somewhat mess up, we both were wrong, and from this day forward, I'll be damn if I continue chasing behind a nigga who was choosing anyway. Then the nigga was choosing down not up. Fuck Marshad! I hope that he finds everything he needed in that grimy, lame hoe.

"I hate you Mora, no wonder Dre killed himself! He didn't want to be with a heartless bitch like you!"

*Damn. Low blow.*

Kamora eyes watered she chuckled and slapped the shit out of Moni. My friend hit the floor. I had tears in my eyes watching my friend breaking down. I had to put my blunt out.

"I love him. I need him. I love him so much!" she repeatedly cried out.

Kamora stood over her with tears in her eyes, yet it was as if she dared those bitches to fall. Hell, even her own tears didn't want no smoke! As she stood with glossy eyes looking at her baby sister, she told Moni some shit that had me instantly thinking about Mars and me.

"You may love that nigga, but it's hella clear that you don't love your fucking self. You don't love him. Hell, your ass doesn't know shit about love! Bringing up my dead husband like you know some shit about Dredon or our connection! Kamoni, I love you baby girl, and that's always. However, watch your mouth, or I will punch you in it." she said with a shaky voice

Moni was crying hard. I went to try to console her but was stopped by Mora's icy ass voice.

"Let her be. She's good."

Taking a deep breath, I just decided to get the fuck out of there. My heart was hurting. Leaving out the building, I wiped the tears from my cheeks. Marshad was still outside, but I didn't want to deal with this shit.

"Come here, Little."

"Leave me alone, Mars. Go be with your girl! I promise I'm done. You want me to leave you alone. You got that!" I said, crying.

"Man, shut up," he said, pinning me to my car.

I couldn't stop the tears. Looking at Marshad, I definitely felt Moni's pain. I love him. It really did seem like he had my heart effortlessly, yet he continually breaks it. He kissed me, and I relaxed. He opened the door to the backseat of my car, laid me down, kissing on my neck and down my body. Moving my skirt up, he moved the black lacy thong away as he fingered my pussy. I moaned out. When his tongue connected with my clit, my head thrashed against my seat. It's been so long since I experienced this feeling, and I missed it. *I missed him!* I came in Mars' mouth, and he licked his lips.

I instantly felt like shit for being weak for this nigga. I pushed him off me and pulled down my skirt. Since it was early morning, nobody was outside. I was tired, a bit tipsy, high, and feeling stupid. Mars kissed my lips softly, sat me in the driver's seat, and pulled my seatbelt over me.

"Drive safe, Little," he said to me and hopped in his car, probably headed back to that whack ass bitch Ana.

I drove my dumb ass home safely like Mars told me beyond ready to give my pillow this head.

# 5

## KYRIE "KY" MIKSON

"U ncle Ky, I miss Lani," Jahanna said, giving me those big pretty eyes. *Man, my niece will always be my heart.*

My twin brother Kyren got jammed up for killing his sidepiece who shot Jahresa, which is baby Jah's mom. The fucked up part is she was aiming for baby girl, and Resa took that bullet like any good mother. How bitter and dick craze does a bitch got to be to be gunning for a one-year-old? I couldn't tell you. All I know is that the bitch took that shot.

Naturally, Resa dove in front of her one-year-old daughter, taking the bullet right to her heart and dying instantly. My brother watched that shit unfold. He immediately pulled out his gat ripping into that hoe's body. He must have filled her up with thirty bullets at minimum. It's sad to say, he was sentenced to life, and they even talking about giving him the death penalty. That shit is so fucking backwards. We're gone kill you for killing somebody.

This government is no different from radical anti-abortion fighters. Muthafuckas were against women "murdering" a baby or fetus but were kidnapping doctors killing them, not to mention blowing up hospitals. The shit is beyond stupid! It is what it is though. I hate to be the nigga unbelieving in change, yet it's too many people in the world who just don't give a fuck, and if they do, it's not nearly enough! I was minding my fucking business getting this money and praying that the system does not murder me. That community-building trying to empower black people who'd rather get defensive than learn some shit was out for your boy. I'm good.

In the meantime, I'm thinking about Luna. She is fine as fuck. She had smooth, chocolate brown skin, was thick, and the way she was with baby girl is admirable. It's hella cute how I make her pretty ass nervous.

"Jahanna, we can go see them tonight. You want to go to Sugar Momma's?" Her eyes lit up.

Sugar Momma is Jahresa's grandmother. That's how I met Kamora and then later Kamoni. Their little brother Kamaal stays with Sugar Momma. He is ten and the little nigga is quiet as hell. He pays attention though. It's clear in his drawings. Little man is the shit, and although I was just a drug dealer/ college nigga, I took that brotherly role when it came to little man.

I'm not gone speak too much on the shit going on with that family, but it's some dysfunctional mess. Kamora is tough love though. Nobody wants to hear her fucking mouth, myself included. Lunya was pushing weed for me whereas Kamoni was a fucking no off rip. First, she was too emotional with her feelings and shit. I understand women were naturally sensitive, but Moni was laid back with a ridiculous emotional quality that makes my balls itch. Don't no man want itchy balls, bro. Second, Kamora's ass wasn't shit nice, especially when it came to her siblings. Yo boy didn't want no heat from that woman. Her nigga had to be a gangsta or a heavy hitta to put up with her, no cap!

I bathed my niece and dressed her in some blue jean overalls shorts and a pink top. I put her socks on with her pink and white Air Max. I wasn't fucking with that hair, so I put it in a bun like I always do. Shit, Jahresa was adamant about strangers in her baby's head. She was borderline homicidal, and although my sister-in-law is resting in peace, I ain't want her knocking shit around my crib hunting me, so hair shops were out!

Matching my niece's fly, I put on blue jean shorts, a white Nike muscle shirt, and my white and black Air Max. My locs were freshly twisted, and my arms were revealing all the artwork decorating my arms. I'm not no bragging ass nigga, so I'll just say this. I will never have an issue with making a woman's pussy wet off looks alone. That's on me.

I put Jah in her car seat and gave her the tablet. Her little self is weird watching other kids play with toys, but shit, as long as my baby is happy, I'm good. Hopping in the black Navigator, I headed to Sugar Momma's place. Man, I love that lady. She was a warrior. I pulled up, parked, grabbed Jah, and headed to the front door. Looking at Sugar Momma, she was beautiful and still looking youthful with a silver-gray afro. She took Jah from me, hugging her tight. They had an unbreakable bond. Jah did not play about her Sugar Momma!

Baylee came up all in my face like usual. She was Jah's auntie and Jahresa little sister. They were only a year apart, and this bitch was nothing like Resa. Jah didn't like her ass for nothing. That was her auntie, yet you would think Kamora and Kamoni were baby girl's aunties. Baylee is grimy as hell, I merch. She got snake tattooed right on her wrist. Shit, I don't give a fuck what her reasoning behind it was. The bitch is a snake.

Jah frowned her little face up as Baylee tried to reach for her, mean ass. It is funny as hell how much she acts like her mom even though she lost her so young. She reminds me so much of Resa's ass. I kissed Sugar Momma and Jah on the cheek before heading back to my car. Of course, Baylee's ass followed right behind me.

"Why you acting like that?"

"You gotta girlfriend, shawty, yeah?"

"What she gotta do with us?" I chuckled.

"You're right. I got shit to do, Baylee. Be cool and tell yo bitch you like dick," I said before hopping in my whip and speeding down the street.

I was meeting that nigga Zeriah at the court and look who I see? Fine ass Luna in her scrubs and a big ass bun on top of her head. Walking to her car, I followed her.

"Ayo, where you going?" I said, licking my lips. She smirked.

"Pick up my daughter. You're my daddy, huh?" I walked up on her.

"Say, I'm trying to be something, shawty."

Her breath got caught. Mane, this shit is fun. Her ass is so responsive.

"I have a nigga," she blurted out, making me laugh.

Fuck dude! I'm not even doing shit to her yet look how she acts. Yeah, this is for sure about to be all me. I will go at her pace for now. Shit, I bet all my fucking bread that the nigga ain't making her feel the shit I would. Ya heard me. I nodded my head and opened her door, getting an eye full of her ass. I was gone slap that shit, yet I already knew she would have a fucking heart attack trying to be loyal to a mark ass fuck nigga. Muthafuckas didn't have to tell me shit. I could tell dude most likely wasn't her one. I didn't even know what the fuck I was gone do with Luna just yet, but I was definitely gone use Jah and Lani's friendship to get closer. Hell, it's for the greater good.

I played a couple of games of twenty-one with Riah, and this hooping ass nigga busted my ass. It was all good. That's my partna for sure. I met that nigga when I used to get tatted by his brother. We also attended the same college until I transferred. I originally stayed in Atlanta until shit went left with Jahresa. I was the godfather, hand-picked by Resa herself. Hell, I was just happy to be the uncle, but Jahresa was dead ass like my sister on some shit. I had taken baby Jah to Atlanta with me when all that shit went down. We just recently moved out here to New Orleans since Resa's people were here. Kyren's stupid ass really had no business...

"Nigga, fuck you were saying to my cousin?" Riah said rudely interrupting my thoughts. He was out of breath and pouring water on his face. I'll take his rude ass over Bear any day though.

"I was trying to see what her ass had going on nigga, fuck outta here," I told him as he laughed.

"Aiight, you know what the fuck it is."

"Shit yeah, I do. Don't worry about my shit, dawg. Kamoni is still running behind that lame ass nigga, so you got your own shit to focus on." He used to talk nonstop about that damn girl. Yes indeed, the one who got away.

"Nigga, you got me fucked up. Moni is doing what I'm letting her do. She ain't ready for a nigga like me the fuck! I'm not playing no games with her. I play for keeps. She needs time with that nigga, that's all! It's no biggie. I'm Gucci!" this lame ass nigga spat with conviction.

"Shut yo stupid ass up talking about no biggie, you Gucci, fuck," I joked. This was my nigga. Since we met, he's been solid. Yes indeed, Riah is my bro.

"Nah, real shit, bih. That's yo partna! I'm taking his bitch. It's over with."

I was cracking up. Zeriah knew damn well that I only fucked with that nigga Cole on a business trip. Nothing more, fuck outta here!

"Whatever bihh, do yo shit," I said.

WE'VE BEEN out for a minute. Looking at my phone, I had no miss calls. Laughing aloud, I thought about how Jah would call my ass every hour all day unless she is with Sugar Momma. I don't hear shit from her. Man, I love my niece so much. We were heading to see Kyren in a couple of days. She adored her daddy. She stayed telling him the slogan we had as kids. *"Chin up, daddy! We are giants."* She told him this after every visit. I know looking at Jah made him feel fucked up about Resa. She was so much like her, it was scary— sweet as hell and transparent, so if she didn't fuck with you, her face, energy, and tone showed. She stood on her decisions. Jah was only four, and she was already like that.

I got the address I needed from Riah before I headed my way and that nigga headed his way. I went home, showered, and got dressed. I had a plan for Luna's sexy ass soon. Kyren called. We talked briefly, but he really wanted to speak to Jah. I told him she was at Sugar Momma's and he immediately ended the call with me to call Sugar Momma. Kyren loves his daughter. That's the only piece of Resa he has left besides the memories. I've told my brother plenty of times that we have to think with our heads, not our dick. I'm not justifying shit that hoe did, but that's my brother, so I let him know he opened the door for that bullshit.

I went to re-up and sent out a group text letting all my workers know that we had more product through the code words we established through my moving company that each technically worked at as a legit front. I was making appointments to have one-on-one sit-downs with my team until I was ready to pick up baby Jah.

After a long day of hard work and dedication, I sat in my whip, counting my bread. I had to make a deposit into all three of baby Jah's bank accounts. I had one last stop before I headed back to Sugar Momma's to pick my baby girl up.

Pulling up at the gravesite, I got out with the white and red roses to lay on Resa's grave. Kamora was sitting there with a big ass bottle of Hennessy talking to her cousin. I stood back listening to her. I didn't want to interrupt.

"Man, Jahresa you really fucked up with it leaving me with these slow ass people, my girl. I miss you so much. Kamoni is fucking up. Baylee is a hot, confusing mess. The only people I like are Maal and baby Jah right now. Oh and Sugar Momma, but you know that's my queen always. Remember when I was dumb in love with Dredon, and yo ass snatched me up by my hair at that barbershop on Highland? I went and made myself look like a weak bitch. Man, I couldn't stand yo ass sometimes, Resa! You were always trying to hold my stupid ass accountable!

Fuck him! Bitch, do you know who you are? The same shit you asked me, I have to ask Moni. Damn, baby! Why you have to leave me like this? First Dredon, then you. I don't want to be out here without yawl, shawty! Why did yo ass abandon me? Why? Why? Why? This shit hurt seeing Moni acting like my dumb ass. I gotta be you! I don't want the fucking position, my girl! Rise yo ass up like they said black Jesus did!"

Mora took a big gulp of the Hennessy.

"Man, then Lunya. Now that girl is love. Kamoni has a true friend in her ass, yes indeed. She is the true definition of my bullshit is your bullshit is *our* bullshit in my Kevin Hart voice. Girl, this little nigga Moni's dumb in love, slapped the shit outta her dick crazed self! I know you in heaven acting like Madea crazy ass in *Diary of Mad Black Woman*. Keep calm, baby. Nya cracked his ass with a bottle in the club! She got that ass smooth together. I know your crazy self is condoning that wild ass behavior. Remember when you thought Dre was beating my ass, but we were actually fucking, and you busted in with the gun drawn ready with baby Jahanna on yo back in that damn baby carrier you loved so much. Crazy ass, you were about to catch a body with my baby cousin sleep on your back! Girl, our ass couldn't even finish fucking after you apologized then turned around to leave. When we saw that damn baby sleep in that damn carrier, we were so joked out. Girl, you were too much bitch! Then your nutty ass went and told Dre your baby would have still slept peacefully since you had a silencer on your piece. Lawd them crazy ass New Yorkers corrupted your ass, and then I go marry one! You and Dredon werked my nerves chileee! I miss yawl so much. How yawl gone just go like this? Both of yawl ditched me!"

Mora was breaking down so bad that she took another swig, and I made my presence known.

"Nigga, I knew you were there. Hell, I was married to a gangsta, and this nut kept me on my toes with her wild shit. I'm just having my time with my guardian angel," Mora said, pointing to the tombstone and putting the bottle up to it before pouring some on the ground in front of it. She took a swing of her bottle. I sat my ass down by her, and when she passed the Henny, I drank some.

"Jah acts just like her crazy ass," I said after some silence.

"Hell yeah, Kamaal adores her cute little self. Resa was his favorite. My heart breaks every time he draws her. He didn't even cry at her funeral. Hell, he didn't even talk to nobody, not even ME! I can't believe it's been three years already, man. It seemed like just yesterday she was sipping on that Merlot in a flute acting ghetto and bougie talking that shit about Kyren and how she will never keep a nigga that don't want to be kept, baking cookies at three in the morning because baby Jah kept her ass up. Little mama had her nerves bad as hell! Baby Jah was such a crybaby that Resa had to smoke a fat wood and then end up with the munchies. That shit was a tradition in our teens. We smoke then bake some cookies, cake, cinnamon buns, hell something! Just know our ass was baking. Resa's stupid ass would be talking about all baby Jahanna did is cry, and she needed to relax. Then the nut gone say she wished that she could smoke her baby's ass out."

I choked. *Hell naw!*

"Mane, what? Resa wanted to get the little baby high?" I was joked the fuck out! Hell nah, what's the number to CPS, bro?

"My boy her ass dead ass didn't know what the fuck to do when Jahanna cried and wouldn't stop. Hell, her ass was damn near crying cussing everybody out for spoiling her fucking baby! She was the main one though. Man, I miss this crazy ass girl," her voice cracked.

Shit was fucked up missing somebody close to you, and Resa was good people mane. I wish she could be here to raise Jah. Hell, I wish my brother never fucked with that crazy...

"I never blamed Kyren," she said, wiping her face. "Like so many niggas who cheat, that muthafucka thinks the shit is normal. We fail to realize just because some shit is common don't mean it should be normalized. I never blamed Ren. He fucked up following that trend! He knew Resa was his one. Hell, that entire situation baffled me. Say, why you think the bitch was gunning for Jah instead of Resa? She couldn't have thought her shit through. However, it was mad clear that the bitch thought getting rid of my little cousin would get her the nigga. Obviously, she was confused about the type of man she was trying to be with. That's how you know the bitch was a downgrade from my cousin. Resa was so unbothered. She was sipping on that wine with her pinky out clutching her imaginary pearls at the hoe's nerves. Man the crazy part is, Resa would take a bullet for anybody she loved. That's just how she was built. Sugar Momma did her shit with this one," she said with her hand resting on the stone.

I dead ass had tears falling. Hell, I loved Resa. She was touched in the head. I didn't know how great she was, not the way Mora was describing. I felt cheated and blessed at the same time. It was a privilege to say I knew her. To be able to say we were cool, and she respected me enough to be responsible for her greatest accomplishment— baby Jah. My ass doesn't know it was weird. It's natural to want to be a part of good ass people. I felt a part of her, and I wasn't going to let her down.

"I'm heading to see that nigga in a couple of days," I told her.

"That's what's up. I visit him when I can. He's a solid nigga. He had to be fucking with this girl! Weak shit made her skin hot! Trust me my stupid ass knew. Baby never let up, but when it's real, you got a Resa! I tried to tell her crazy ass violence doesn't solve problems! Now, look at me. I was gone fuck Kamoni up just like Resa did me. Hell, I ain't want to be getting my ass beat. Black kids are so strong-willed and powerful you gotta show that ass where it comes from every now and again so that they get they shit together! Don't be scared to hurt some feelings when they ain't moving right! The ass whoopings we give is love way different than the beatings our ancestors took.

That's hate don't confuse the two. We had to be taught how to hate like that. We were never hateful or malicious. At our core, we had to learn that shit to survive. Generational slavery? Divided? Jealous of one another? Shit no! All humans are all fucked up, and that's facts! Say, some white people are still extremely heartless and comfortable justifying the torturous reality of our history, which has taught us every fucked up quality about the black community. Shit be so fucked up, but I'm not even gone get into that all deep since I already know how your ass is!"

She laughed, and so did I. Getting up I hugged Mora. I looked at the bottle then her.

"Baby, I'm good. I don't get drunk. I'm a lady!" she said, smiling at Resa.

I laughed and shook my head. I headed to my car to go pick up Jah and then to the address Riah gave me earlier.

# 6

## LUNYA

It was movie night. We usually have it at my parents, but my dad basically put us out trying to do something special for my mom. She says we are spoiled. He done took her on two trips, and we're not even done with July. Now we're getting kicked out. I love my parents' bond. They were black love, and I was here for it.

The summer semester had ended. I was so happy, but it was short lived since fall was gone be here quicker than I could prepare myself for. I was sad as hell about Marshad today. Like I told him, he was gone be mine. I knew since I was thirteen that I would have his kids. He was pissing me off with this hot and cold shit. Fuck Ana. The bitch was still getting fucked by Skype while Mars wants to go to bat for the bitch. Like boy pay attention. I, for one, am not saying shit. That's his business. He clearly wanted to learn the hard way. I told his ass he was mine and that should of let him know right there that he needed to drop ole girl. I know I haven't been clear about the incident that brings us to the current situation I have with Mars. I'm just gone run it real quick!

Marshad took my virginity in high school. I was sixteen, and he was nineteen. My love runs deep for Mars. Nobody but Luna knows about the situation I had with Mars during my junior year in high school. We weren't together. I didn't tell Marshad I was a virgin the first time we had sex. When he found out he was indeed my first, after being confronted by Luna, he told me not to get confused. We were just having fun. Of course, this hurt my feelings, mainly because he was messing around with other females right in my face. Since he was having his fun, I matched his energy.

I met Skype walking home from school one day. Usually, I didn't entertain other niggas. However, Skype was fine, and Marshad had me fucked up. I decided to date Skype while still having sex with Mars. Skype was cool, we went out often, and he picked me up from school daily. I never had sex with Skype! He eats the box from time to time, but that's all. If I wasn't clear before I'm going to say it again. Only ONE nigga has had the privilege of having sex with me, and his name is MARSHAD Leroy HUDSON!

When Mars found out about my connection with Skype, he was pissed! I was all types of hoes, and he was hurt. I didn't get it, who the hell did he think he was? I was not about to beg that nigga to do right. He was angry that a bitch wasn't sweating him after he embarrassed the hell out of me. No man will have me that pressed to play in my face and think I'm not gone play back! I knew that even at sixteen. So, you fucking right, I amped up the situation with Skype to Mars. He wasn't about to keep playing me stupid.

The issue came when I had the most embarrassing situation go down right in the hallways of my school and then later at a neighborhood house party.

"Where's the little bitch at, SKYLOU! I mean yawl been messing around, right?" Ana screamed, trying to bypass Skype.

I was coming out of my last class and didn't even notice a pissed off Ana as I saw the man that has been spending time and money on me for the last six to seven months. I smiled at him, and she saw it.

"Is this the young bitch?" Ana yelled, pinning me with a pissed off expression, which caused me to frown instantly. I looked at Skype, and guilt covered his face.

"Excuse you, baby?" I said beyond confused but not about to let nobody disrespect me.

"Little bitch don't speak, I know you not the young bitch fucking MY nigga!" she screamed,

I didn't know what the fuck this hoe was talking about, but she had me all wrong if she thought she was gone be talking to me crazy! She spat on me, and next thing I knew, I was flying across Skype to beat that ass. I had Ana by the hair and was being pulled by security, but I refused to let her ass go. I didn't give not one fuck about shit. I was a straight-A student, on the honor roll, and in the hallways fucking Ana ass up for putting her spit on me. I got suspended, and Luca had to pick me up from the juvenile detention center. Ana was really trying to press charges like she had a right to bring her grown ass to my high school! I listened to Skype for months after that when he said it wasn't shit with them.

We continued like shit was all good until I got caught up with Skype by Mars.

We were all partying after a school dance. I had been stopped worrying about Mars whereabouts, but this particular night I should have been. As I turned up with Skype shaking my ass and having a good ass time, Mars snatched my ass up at that party. I was drunk as hell and didn't give a fuck. We had a huge argument a few hours before my dance because he thought it was okay to bring a bitch to my parents' house when he went to meet Luca. I was pissed, but of course, I couldn't trip since I wasn't even supposed to be fucking with him. Had my brother found that shit out he would have killed Mars and beat my ass. I had to be cool, so I was, but baby, you better believe I sent a text and cussed his as clean the fuck out. Then I went out with Skype to help me deal with my hurt feelings.

The nigga who party it was knew Mars and invited him. I ignored Mars and didn't expect him to act a fool since he knew damn well we were not even together like I'm out doing me and he forgets all about that "we just having fun" shit he tried spinning me.

Dragging me upstairs, he slammed the door.

"Fuck is you doing? You really that pissed you fucking other niggas?" he barked.

"Nigga, wwhhat?" I slurred my words, too drunk.

"Mane, you a little ass girl! I don't know how you thought you could ever be my bitch!" he spat.

"Fuck you! I don't want to be shit to you!" I said with tears flooding to the rim of my eyes.

"Ha, now you want to cry and shit like you wasn't just shaking yo ass for the next nigga. I should have known your ass was just a spoiled little hoe!" He chuckled.

"It's cool, Little. I just got one question! Were you even a virgin or was that just some bullshit?"

"Nigga, fuck YOU!"

"Never again, baby! My dick don't fuck thots!" he spat and stormed out of the room.

I had to get myself together. I returned to the party. Ready to go, I looked around for Skype and couldn't find him anywhere. Giving up my search, I walked into the bathroom since I wasn't feeling well. Opening the bathroom door, I was greeted by Skype getting his dick sucked by Ana. I was sick to my stomach and threw up all the food and liquor I had consumed. I ran out of there as quickly as I busted in, and Skype ran after me trying to apologize.

That was the end of both situationships for me. Skype was still fucking with his baby mama, and Marshad hated my ass.

THERE WAS REALLY no smoke with Ana on my end. I thought she was just the baby mom. Marshad was playing games, and Skype was there. Hell, that nigga Skype picked me up from school faithfully, eat my pussy all the time, and stayed giving me money. He was the perfect distraction without the sex. Till this day, only one nigga had the luxury of having sex with me, and the nigga acted like I'm the toddler bitch his stupid ass lady loved to call me.

My bad, my girl! Shit, the head was good, and I was broke hell. I ain't know yawl was a "family."

I mean, I eventually gave the nigga back, and now the same bitch got the man that I'm so in love with. Ain't karma a comical, sexy drag bitch?

I received a call from my old roommate. She finished the spring semester and took her ass back to Chicago with her man. They were too cute, and I can't wait to visit.

"Sway, do the thing I like. Nah, the other thing, boy hold on," Ivory said.

"Hey, Nya, boo! When are you going to visit, hoe?"

"Fall break? It's up to you, miss."

"Mmm, fuck yeah, that thing!" she moaned. Gurllll, I know you fucking lying!

"Byeeee, Ivory, call me back, hoe." I laughed and clicked on her ass. She gone call me knowing she was busy.

Sway was just a smooth ass nigga. Honestly, he was boyfriend goals. His right hand, Brasi had been heavily on my mind. He was a fine, chocolate nigga, and no lie, when I visit, I might actually give him a real chance. With the way that shit's been going with Marshad, maybe I did just need to let his ass go.

Brasi was texting me a little more than usual since he knew I was coming in town for fall break. He almost got me the last time he came in town with Sway back when Ivory was here. Matter fact, every time the nigga visited, he took my mind off Mars.

Kamoni still hasn't returned any of my calls, which had me feeling like fuck her. I didn't do shit to her. I'm going to mind my fucking business from now on. I don't care what that nigga do to her. Hell, ignoring me and shit, and I could be dead somewhere, snatched up and calling her.

I took my last exam and headed to pick up Lani from my mom's job. Amod had her while Luna worked but dropped her off early. My mom had gotten stuck at work. I was rushing and shit, but once I got there, my mom told me Luna left work early to come to get my Pooh.

"What you got on? Little girl, you are showing too much cleavage!" *Like how? I barely have titties!*

I was feeling cute in the short, distressed booty shorts with the pockets hanging out the bottom, which I paired with a white V-neck with the word *Solid* on the front in black lettering. I had some sparkly silver slides on my feet. My locs were in a cute updo. I had big silver hoops in my ear, and my lips were glossy. Not really in the mood to go back and forth with Nubia, I told her I loved her and got the fuck on.

Leaving out of the natural hair shop that she owned, I decided to take myself on a date. I was gone go eat at the steak house, get a massage, and afterwards, I would head to Luca and Dimes.

I sat at the table and ordered myself a steak and cheesy mashed potatoes with asparagus on the side. I was scrolling my Instagram and enjoying myself as well as my food when the voice of the nigga who started the whole incident back in high school made himself present. I heard Skype's voice close to me. He is fine as hell, light skin, with pretty ass light brown eyes. We were still cool. I knew I could get that whenever! Hell, he didn't even stop fucking with me, but when everything went down, and it was revealed that he was indeed in a relationship with that damn girl, I dipped out on his ass. He's still my boy though.

"Why is your fine ass sitting alone?" he asked me.

"I'm enjoying myself. Who are you here with? I don't want any drama Skylou," I said blasting his birth name.

"Ana's in the car, shawty. It's good. You know if your ass didn't cut a nigga off, you could be a nigga wife by now. My moms asked about you." He licked his lips as I shook my head.

He is such a dog, and I knew Ana's stupid ass wasn't giving up Skype. Mars was definitely getting played on, but I was gone mind my business. I dismissed Skype. He was cool people, but he is such a slut that it wasn't even funny. He will never get my cookies, not in high school and damn sure not now. As fine as he is, that dog shit he's on just turns me off. He is older, and he is paid, yet his bread didn't impress me— not then and damn sure not now.

I made my own money, and my parents and older brother would give me the world if I asked them for it. Skype was a good friend, but let him tell it he was just playing that position until I'm ready to be with him. I wasn't on that kick with him anymore though. I learned my lesson with the incident in high school. Marshad was pissed when he found out about me messing with Skype. Getting my revenge and trying to show Mars that I wasn't a little ass girl is why

Marshad stays capping like it's nothing with us. At the end of the day, Skype and I will never be, not sexually or shit else, just homies that's it.

"Well, get back to her," I told him while texting Kyrie about my pack.

I couldn't help my mind from wondering to Marshad, I wanted to tell the man about what his little bitch had been up to, but to be real that shit wasn't my place. I meant what I said about being done with his bullshit. There was no need for me to throw salt on that thotivity Ana had going on. Hell, Mars is not fucking with me. He is definitely playing games with me as Dime said. I was over Mars' foolishness, and his bullshit is below me. I didn't want to keep chasing his ass, so I wouldn't.

Skype gave me a stack and told me to hit him up when I had free time to spare. I was not doing that shit. It was over with for him and me with his hoe ass, not to mention he's *still* messing with Ana. Yeah, he put a nail in the coffin with us. I'm moving on to bigger and better things. I was about to be a sophomore in college. I was nowhere near on the same kick as back when I was dealing with Skype to piss Mars off, especially after Mars took my virginity, and then had the nerves to label me a hoe. Marshad basically said fuck me talking about it was a mistake and how he shouldn't have crossed those lines because I don't understand the meaning of a good time.

All I wanted was Marshad. If I couldn't have him like I wanted, I was going to move forward, never backwards. Skype was for sure wasting his time if he wanted more than the casual friendship we developed after I stopped fucking around with him. He leaned down kissing my cheek before leaving out.

Enjoying my medium rare steak as well as my mashed potatoes and vegetables, I had a virgin daiquiri since I forgot my fake ID in my dorm room. After a bomb ass lunch date with myself, my massage was up next. Deciding to be the bigger person since losing a good friend, especially my best friend, is not an option. I stopped by Kamoni's to offer her to go. I really wanted to be here for her. Then again, she wasn't allowing that because of how I reacted to that punk ass nigga Cole slapping her. I didn't know exactly how she expected me to watch this nigga treat her like shit, mainly because I was a real ass friend. Regardless of her decisions, bad or good, I wanted to be there for her, and without a doubt, I was going to be.

I used my key to enter her house, and Cole was fucking some skinny white bitch in my friend's crib. I shook my head. I started dialing her number. As the phone rang for the third time, she walked in. She looked numb, yet when she spit the razer from under her tongue, slicing the bitch, I pulled my small .22 aiming at Cole daring him to jump stupid. I did not like his ass on no level anyway.

I understood that he did my girl so dirty only because she allowed it. However, I still felt like the nigga was foul as hell to be pulling the shit he been doing to my girl— fuck nigga. Any good friend would be protective of their friends, so naturally, I wanted to protect Moni. At the same time, I was putting myself at risk by trying to do so. Kamoni beat the fuck out of the Hillary Duff look alike. She was stupid thick with hips and ass. After Kamoni beat the girl up, she moved on to Cole. He looked unbothered until his lip got split by the punch she gave him to the mouth.

"Nigga, how you gone be fucking a bitch in my house?" she said, swinging on him again and busting his nose.

It must have been the conviction in that punch that kicked his reflexes into action to hit her ass back, which instantly caused me to shoot his ass in the foot. Cursing, he hopped towards me. I was about to shoot that nigga again, but Moni stood in front of me.

"Just leave Lunya I got this!" she screamed at me.

This couldn't be real. I was passed over this dumb shit and the fact that Moni seriously felt the need to keep defending this nigga. She should have let me take the shot. I felt so played that I knew if I didn't remove myself, I was gone be in this bitch fighting my best friend. I am leaving just like she said. I was pissed and feeling like a duck for getting involved at all. This is the last time I go to bat for this bitch just to be looking like the leading clown in Kamoni's circus for trying to help. I was over the bullshit. It is officially fuck Kamoni at this point. If her heart was set and truly content with being a weak hoe, then who was I to not let her be a stupid bitch in peace?

No longer up for a massage, I picked up my pack from Kyrie and headed to my brother's house. I pulled up, parked my car, and headed inside after using my key to get inside. I loved this mansion so much. Hell, Diamond's ass will let me move in. All I had to do was ask.

My heart was heavy as hell as I entered my brothers beautiful home. Dime was in the kitchen smelling some pretty ass rainbow roses in a black silk robe, and her hair was in a bun on top of her head. She had a mango chiller smoothie from Smoothie King, and she was glowing. I swear my baby niece is going to be gorgeous. I greeted her, and after telling her all the shit that went down, I felt a tad bit better.

It was close to six p.m. when Luna and Lani came inside along with Kamora. We all sat talking to each other. Mora had a long-stemmed red single rose and a note that she immediately handed to Dime.

"It's nice to finally meet you. I'm Kamora. Luca has paid me to do your hair and makeup."

Diamond was blushing hard as she read the note. She rushed off to get dressed, and I sat talking to Mora about school and my future plans. I decided to not bring up the situation with Moni to her. We sipped on red wine as Mora prepared Dime for her date. Luna and Alani went upstairs, and I ducked off in the bathroom to change into some night shorts and a long sleeve t-shirt. I also had put on my fuzzy, purple socks. I then went into the kitchen to put the pizza in the oven and make homemade hot wings. As I prepared for the movie night that my sister and pooh was having, I received a long ass text from Kamoni that would change the dynamics of our friendship forever.

**Kamoni:** *We just need some space in our friendship. It seems as if you have no respect for my relationship. I am a grown ass woman. I don't need you stepping out of your lane, telling me about my man, or telling my older* *sister about my shit like I am a little ass kid! What goes on between my dude and me is our business. Since you clearly don't know how to be a friend, let's just put a pause on our friendship. When you can stop stepping into my business, maybe we can be friends again! Until then, I am just going to wish you the best. I know your intentions are good, Nya. I just will not continue to add more friction to my relationship than it already is behind your actions. You are my friend, and I love you always for your protection, but I don't need you popping off on my man. I got this! I wish you well love.*

**Me:** *Bet!*

I didn't really give a fuck about what she was saying. I will never sit back and watch my friend get handled fucked up. Yet, I would be lying if I said that this shit didn't hurt me. I started popping the popcorn and cooking the hot wings as tears slid down my cheeks. I was crying about the situation because I couldn't believe after all the shit we been through together that it could be so easy for Moni to end our friendship over a scrub ass nigga. Diamond came looking stunning. After telling her about the reasoning for the tears sliding down my cheeks and the pain currently gripping my heart, Dime looked me in my face and took a deep breath.

"Listen, I wouldn't be me if I didn't give the hard knock truth, so listen to me and please don't take anything I say the wrong way. I promise you I'm only telling you because I care. The only person I feel the need to advise in some shit is Rayna, but we have grown close. Nya, you are my girl, and I love you boo, *but* yo ass is working my nerves with all this weak shit, baby. It's okay. I get it. Shit hurts, and it's gone hurt but fuck them! Him, her, that, this, fuck it! I know girl, trust me. I've been you. It's harder than one two done. If you don't start saying fuck them to the people trying they best to hold you back and dimming your brightness, you are not gone make it, boo.

Women like you and me are built for fucking pressure. It hurts. I felt knives in my back that left me paralyzed wondering why me. I was broken I couldn't seem to stop asking why, and I was worried about the wrong shit instead of declaring that it won't be me anymore! I am not trying to hurt your feelings, boo. I'm giving you the real. Kamoni is going through her shit, and as her friend, you need to let her do that, especially when you're not doing any better. Love yourself. I promise you that the pain you're feeling is temporary. You are strong enough to overcome hurdles even with gun wounds, torment, and being blood-soaked and unprotected. That's our charge as black women. You better know you *will* sustain the storm, so let it fucking pour! Embrace that hurt and figure out what you need to do to overcome that pain. It's on my heart to talk to you just like this. I promise I've been there. I can bless you with this speech knowing that if you take it in and let it build you like it's meant to do, there is no stopping you, my baby.

People are gone hate you because they're not you. They gone take the easy way out when they hurt you. That's because we all got demons we're fighting. It's a fact that some people hearts are just better than others. Some people are stronger than others. Let it go and let God. Embrace the universe and that higher power that keeps you winning. Fuck them critics and toxics up with your success! Muthafuckas hate to witness you flourishing after they fucked over you. Most people don't have the mental capacity to know what that self-love is about. Hell, when you know your worth, you open the doors quick for the people who counted you out. You got this, my girl, now let me go meet your fine ass brother!"

I hurriedly wiped my eyes as Luna and Lani came down the stairs in their pajamas and into the kitchen.

"Sparklyyy, you pretty," Alani told Dime as she ran up to her, Dime scooped her up hugging her tight as she responded to her, "Noooo princess Lani, you're pretty."

I smiled. Alani wasn't lying. Diamond was beautiful. She had on a black lace dress, and her baby bump was so cute. The lace front Kamora had done for her was laid! Deep burgundy lipstick adored her full lips, and the red roses tatted on her shoulder complimented the long-stemmed, single rose that my brother sent her. His ass was working overtime to get out of the dog house! Happy wife happy life is engraved in Luca for sure. Our dad wasn't for none. There shall be no frown on his queen's face. Luke Micah Wright is the first man who has ever had my heart. The part that belongs to my daddy will forever be his. I am a daddy's girl for life!

Diamond and Mora left, and Luna, Lani, and I sat watching The *Lion King* for the hundredth time. I swear my entire soul can't stand Luna ass for putting Lani on to this movie. This is all we will watch day in and out, like damn, at least let's watch part two! There wasn't shit wrong with Kiara, yet Alani just loves Simba when he was little. She cries real tears every single time Simba finds his father's body. It's really not funny, yet the way Alani acts heartbroken as if she didn't know what was gone happen every single time, I swear her little ass better be an actor.

Pulling out my phone, I received a text from Marshad. I wanted to ignore him, but I low key missed the man, so I hit his ass back! I was still salty about how shit went down with Kamoni, but at the same time, look at me entertaining this nigga when he with that girl. Fuck her, is how I felt, yet I was looking at myself like bitch you mad at Moni though. I don't play second to anybody, hell I came out my mama pussy first! That's exactly why...

"Yo ass a clown if you let Mars pick you up after the way he handled you," Luna said all in my phone.

"Damn, siblings don't mind they damn business like they used to."

"Gurllll, shut up. You letting that man play you out, and for what?"

I guess she thinks she is looking in the mirror today, but I'm not gone hop on her ass. She clearly has something to let off her chest. I'm gone let her speak. Not every disagreement is an argument. Only muthafuckas who don't care about your feelings think that they have to talk shit to get their point across.

"What you mean, Lunatic?" I referred to her by this name when she was blowing me and sometimes just to fuck with her. She hated it! Like any other sister, I like getting on my siblings' nerves every now and again.

"I mean, LUNYA," she started in her patient voice. I grinned. My sister is dope.

"Marshad treats you fucked up! Baby, you're a queen, and if you keep letting that nigga treat you fucked up, I'm telling dad you out here acting fatherless looking for love in the wrong places!"

"I'm good. Let me handle my shit with Mars. What's up with you and my boy?" I wanted to know.

"Nah, slick, we talking about you," she said, unable to contain her smile.

Alani had passed out. Another interesting fact about my Pooh is her ass will be up one minute and be out the next as if she is pushing a nine to five and on her feet all day.

"Luna, YOU! You cheating on Mod!" I said.

"I am not, I'm just... keeping my options open. Kyrie is so damn cool though. The fact that he is taking care of his niece until his brother gets out of jail got me looking at him like the heart eyes emoji. He's bae as fuck. Amod is—"

There was a knock at the door cutting her off.

I hopped up to get it. Opening the door, it turned out to be Kyrie with a sleeping Jahanna. She had talked this man right up. Allowing him inside, he followed me to the living room. I looked at Luna as Ky laid baby girl on the couch next to Alani. With the way that Luna was looking in her Nike sweats and big t-shirt with her nappy, thick mane all over her head stuffing popcorn in her mouth, she definitely couldn't have known the nigga was coming.

"Zeriah gave me the information to where you were at. Let me talk to you for a minute," he said to her. Luna got up, and they went upstairs.

Riah ass is toe the hell up. He could have sent her a heads up. My older cousin Zeriah is down here for the summer going through training and conditioning for the upcoming basketball season. Before my uncle NuZy died, which is my cousins Zyair and Zeriah father and my mother's twin brother, he was a basketball player growing up and could have gone pro. He taught Luca everything he knew. Ball was literally life For Lu until my uncle died. Once Luca lost his jersey, he didn't play at all. Riah has always been interested, so it was only right for Luca to train him since my uncle taught him so much before he died.

I cuddled up next to the girls. Deciding to text Mars, I said never mind. He responded with bet. I allowed the tears to slide down my cheeks as I wondered why I wanted to be with a nigga who clearly didn't want to be with me. His ass was playing games where I had real love. Marshad was the first person I ever had sex with. It baffled the fuck out of me how he wanted to act like I was crazy when he turned my little ass out at sixteen! Every man I come across automatically gets compared to him. This whole situation is a never-ending headache. It's my fault though.

# 7

# LUNA

"What you doing here, Ky?" I asked a bit self-conscious.

He popped up on me for real. I was definitely in my natural state, and my hair was all over the place. I had on my pajamas, but the way he was standing here looking at me had me feeling like I am the prettiest girl in the world. I just loved the way he made me feel. He was for sure conjuring up feelings that I knew shouldn't be here, especially since I'm trying with Amod. Right? I am in love with my baby's dad, yet this man in front of me had me so unsure.

"We missed yawl, shawty," he answered me, pulling me close and making the butterflies in my stomach flutter even more.

"Is that right?" I smiled at him.

"Seriously, baby. Jah was like where's Lani, and I'm like, where's my shawty?"

"I'm not your shawty, Kyrie. I have a man," I told him knowing the words sounded official, but my energy wasn't matching it.

I am feeling Kyrie something serious, but I wanted my family to work. Hell, I need it to work. I had to try again this last time, if not for me for Alani. Holding my head up, I looked into Kyrie's eyes and decided to be real with him.

"Look, Ky. I like you, but I'm trying to see if my baby daddy will work and if we can do the family thing. You're a distraction to that goal that I have for myself. I can't do this with you," I told him, trying to remove myself from his arms.

"I understand, love, but at the same time. I don't really care about none of that shit. We can chill, and you can force that situation with Alani's dad if that's what you want. Regardless of our situation, your daughter and my niece are besties, so for their sake, we will just keep this platonic," he said backing up, making me immediately miss his warmth.

"Thank you," I told him.

"After this, yo fine ass is just my dawg," he stated and kissed me so passionately that all I could think about is him kissing my second pair of lips.

Once he broke the kiss, he headed out. Stopping at the door, he asked if Jah could stay here with Alani, I agreed due to Alani's bugging my ass all day about her bestie. I was all hot and bothered now. I needed to talk but didn't have many friends outside my sister and her best friend, Kamoni. I didn't want to discuss the situation with Nya since she is bias, and Kamoni was out since she into it with Nya and dealing with her own drama. Needing to vent, I made decided to hit up Rayna. She was out in Atlanta with my cousin, but we clicked! She babysat Alani a few times, we did lunch, and my cousin is so in love with her it's ridiculous, which is how I got to know her so well.

My brother and older cousin are not against using Nya and me to their benefit with Rae and Dime. That's exactly what Zy did when he got jammed up with a Bella, Brianna, or Bianca? Hell, I don't remember the damn girl's name, but she was a pretty Spanish chick, and I was minding my own business when the girl came up trying to check Rae at this seafood restaurant that I invited Rae to. I couldn't believe Rayna has never eaten crawfish.

I was running late, and Diamond had a doctor's appointment, so Rayna ended up watching Alani. I decided to treat her for watching my baby last minute. She didn't have to do that, although she told my ass I was tripping for wanting to do something nice. She eventually gave in taking me up on my offer. The Spanish chick was on some other shit, so I called my cousin. He was at the house with Alani. He had pulled up to Dime and Lucas when I did. He offered to watch Alani after Rae made me beg her ass to let me take her out to eat.

Long story short, Rayna's temper is out of control! She beat the fuck out of the girl, and we fled the restaurant before the cops came. We didn't go back to the house. She was pissed off! Her phone kept ringing, and she just sang along to the ringtone she quickly set to my cousin's calls too. It was no longer "Ride For Me" by Anne Marie. It was replaced with Drake's "Mob Ties" song, and she was screaming the lyrics from her heart while speeding through the streets. I was terrified by her driving. Call me extra, but I was praying to God that everybody on the road made it to their destination safe, most importantly myself. I needed to get back to my baby alive.

I knew she was on good bullshit when we pulled up at Bears Print, my cousin's tattoo shop in New Orleans. He also had a location in Baton Rouge and Atlanta. I tried to reason with her, but she wasn't having it, so when my cousin called, I immediately answered the phone. Once she parked, I snatched the keys out the ignition. I didn't know what the fuck she was about to do, but by the way that she just tore up that restaurant, I knew she had some evil ass intentions.

My cousin had to break every speed law there was because after the fourth back and forth of Rayna and me locking and unlocking the car door, he was pulling up. He was pissed. I guess overacting with a splash of petty seems to be a trait that they both share. He had hopped out of his car, leaving Alani in the back seat to deal with a fiery, pissed off Rayna. I jumped out of her car quick, rushing to my cousin's car to hug my daughter. I wasn't driving anywhere else with Rae.

Fuck all that, my heart was beating fast just thinking about the shit. Although she won't be driving me anywhere else, she was cool as hell with a ridiculous mouth, but she is real, so I didn't mind it. From that day forward, we have become close. We talk on the phone often, and she adored my daughter. I was proud of my cousin. He had definitely met his match with that one.

"Hey Luna baby, what's up boo?" she answered on the second ring.

"I just needed to vent to someone real quick. Are you busy?"

"Too busy for you not at all. What's up?" I ran down the situation with Amod, Kyrie, and me, explaining the dilemma.

"From my experience, I know forcing a situation is not going to benefit you. Matter fact, the longer you put up with bullshit, the more bullshit gone come about. When you with a man that is comfortable disrespecting you, and you make excuses for their actions. Pain is what you have to look forward to. I understand you want to make your family work for the sake of Alani, but what exactly are you striving to teach your daughter about love, happiness, and respect? Only you, as a mother, can answer that question. Also, is that nigga an asset or a liability? What are you worth? What type of woman are you and want to be? The answer to those questions can potentially help you with this situation. It's not about Amod or Kyrie. It's not even about Alani. What will make YOU your best self? What makes you happy? You don't owe Amod your love, loyalty, or anything other than an open and clear path to the child that yawl share. In my opinion, you know the answers to the questions I've asked. I promise once you seriously think about them, the solution will smack you in the head."

After chatting with Rayna a bit more about the situation and then her upcoming showcase that I would definitely be attending, we hung up, and I thought over the questions she asked. I still felt like working things out with Amod, and although I am attracted to Kyrie, we were going to keep things platonic between us like he said.

I headed downstairs. Lunya was passed out on the couch next to the girls who were also sleeping. I threw a pillow at Nya waking her up, knowing her ass had a blunt. I don't even smoke weed all like that, but I needed to get my mind right. She woke up mugging me. Knowing she was about to spazz, I quickly shook my head whispering "bitch" and pointed at the sleeping girls next to her. I felt the pettiness in her spirit as she looked at the girls debating if she wanted to wake their butts up in spite of me. I released a deep breath when she just got up and walked towards me, shoving me out of her way as she went into the bathroom.

I wasted no time scooping baby Jah up first not knowing if she sleeps like the dead like Alani or not. I brought her upstairs in the guest room that I claimed as mine and went back downstairs to get my baby. I picked her up and walked to the bottom of the stairs heading upstairs to place her in the room with Jahanna. After making sure they were okay, I headed back downstairs. Lunya was rolling a blunt in the kitchen, so I made my way to her. Now any other time I would talk my shit since she called herself being a drug dealer, selling weed and shit, but I was gone shut my ass up so that I could get high.

"I see how you eyeballing my blunt, and all I know is you bet not start tripping. This is some pressure," she said, drying the blunt with her torch lighter.

I wasn't even offended since I do trip sometimes, so I just waited for her to pass it. I wanted to ask her about Moni. I saw her rushing to wipe her tears when she was talking to Dime, and I was just curious. I know my sister. She always wants to play this hard role like nothing fazes her, but she is soft as shit and kind of slow too if you ask me. The way she is letting Marshad do her just seemed so out of character for her. I'm typically the one making excuses for these niggas, not Nya Ms. Get Money Fuck Niggas.

I knew Mars was different though. He was her first. The first dude to eat that cat and eat it "stupendously" her words at sixteen, not mine! He taught her everything she knows to please him. Of course, my sister and I are close. We shared a womb for nine and a half months. I knew all the tea when it came to my twin. Mars stopped fucking with her when he found out that she was entertaining another nigga. He was clearly sleeping on a sixteen-year-old Nya. She wasn't for none of that shit Mars had going on, especially back then.

I remember like yesterday her patting my baby's back a little too hard for my comfort trying to burp Lani as she vented about how he got her confused with a "ditzy bitch" when he made it clear that they were not together and just having fun. Man, he had the right one with that bullshit because Lunya is Petty Betty for real. She spat "fun" as baby Alani finally burped, and I hurriedly reached for my baby before I was beating Nya's ass. I would never forget that day since I was just waiting to hear a whisper of a cry from my child to fuck my sister up for beating my baby's back. It's funny to me now since I realize it was just new mom syndrome, but I still got the shit bad.

Reaching for the blunt, I took a pull inhaling and instantly felt the effects of the bomb ass green. She definitely had some pressure.

"What's good with you and Moni?" I asked.

"Not shit. She's on her dumb shit, so I'm gone let her be her best self and mind my business. Say, I'm heading to Chicago for fall break. Are you trying to come?"

"That was smooth how you changed the subject, and you already know I'm not leaving Alani to cut up with you and Ivory. Yawl bitches be on yawl bullshit when yawl link up."

"Stop playing, ma could watch Alani, and you know she will," she said.

"Ummm mommy is not always obligated to watch Alani, so shut that shit up. You don't know what she got going on, and you're just volunteering her to babysit like she an in house nanny or something." I was really offended. She got my mama messed up.

"We talked abou—"

"WE didn't talk about shit. There was no agreement to nothing YOU said so no. Just because we conversed, it doesn't mean there was a mutual understanding. Matter fact, it was a disagreement, and just because you initiated the conversation don't mean shit."

Jesus, she really knows how to blow somebody high with that mental she's got. I hit the bunt several more times before passing.

"So, you mad or nah?"

"Yeah, bitch, I am because something is wrong with you. Dad dropped you on your head and didn't tell nobody."

"Don't do me or my daddy!"

"Don't do me or my mama!"

"Anywayyyyyy, what did Kyrie want, and how you end up with baby Jah?"

"How you know Jahanna?"

"That's Kamora and Moni little cousin, remember Jahresa?"

My eyes got big. Jahresa was so full of love, but man, she was crazy as hell. When she was killed, muthafuckas went off. I didn't know she had a child, but I wouldn't since I was in the house being a teen mom around that time. I heard about her death though. The shit was way fucked up.

"Well, that's her daughter. You don't know Kyren, but he is baby Jah's father, and Kyrie is his twin brother."

It all started making sense and coming back. Kyren was the one who got locked up after he killed the hoe who killed Jahresa. Another reason why the city went crazy after her death was due to the books being thrown at Kyren's ass. The law system is so fucked up. The police kill a black man or woman out of fear or hatred and get paid leave, but a black man killing a woman who murdered his ole lady receives a life sentence and possibly death row. It makes no sense, but then again, I know my history, so it actually does. I was high as hell after smoking two blunts. I heard a boom, so I jumped.

"Say, you heard that yeah?"

"No bitch, I did not," Nya said, taking the end piece of the blunt from me.

Hell, I heard it again, so I hopped up quickly, grabbed the broom, and sprinted out the kitchen to the stairs. As I ran up the stairs, I was skipping steps and everything like I was on a kiss good-night mission. You couldn't tell me shit. I heard a boom, and I was determined to get to the girls. There was a little Barbie car in the hall, so I leaped over it and proceeded to the room where the girls were. Opening the door quietly like the assassin I channeled, I was ready to rock something to sleep. But as I opened the door, only the girls were there peacefully sleeping like I left them. I knew damn well I heard a boom, so I was about to access the situation further and look under the bed when I was snatched back by my oversized shirt. Ready for whatever since I knew I heard some shit, I lifted the broom, but it was snatched from me as the bedroom door was pulled shut.

"Girl, bring yo stupid ass back downstairs before you wake them babies up," Nya said, whispering with the broom in her hand now.

"So, you didn't hear a boom?" I asked, feeling dumb.

"Luna, don't ask to smoke my weed again son, for real fuck," Nya said, walking away downstairs, shaking her head.

I peeked back on the girl before following behind her. Once downstairs, I headed back to the kitchen. Lunya had taken out a Walmart Italian sausage pizza. We had long ago smashed the pizza and wings that she made for movie night. I went to the snack cabinet and grabbed a couple of bags of small chips and some fruit snacks as she took out the chocolate chip Pillsbury cookies to bake. I went into the living room to put a movie on and eat my snacks.

Opening the cool ranch Doritos, I got a text from Amod. Ignoring the text, I called him since he went joyriding in my car again after dropping Lani off to my mom causing me to get off early since I didn't want my mom having to balance working and looking after my baby. Although I could have left Alani at the shop with my mom, I was too pissed off to do that shit. That nigga had my car causing me to have to get a ride from my co-worker. Determined not to blow my high, I focused on picking a movie. I clicked on *True To The Game* one of my favorites on Netflix. Although the movie was trash compared to the book, it typically always go down like that. I still like the movie.

"Awe naw, my girl, we done watched this movie to many times I'm sick of it. That's why Alani think watching the same movie back to back is okay. Let's watch *Friday*."

"Nya what the hell? No, we not watching *Friday* if your reasoning behind us not watching this movie is we saw it too many times. That shit makes no sense. This why I don't like you."

"First of all, we can watch three *Friday* movies, and it's *Friday*, a classic. Plus, we can switch it up."

"I'm sick of *Friday*," I said.

"Liessss! Who gets sick of *Friday*? Get out my brother and sister's house, ole disrespectful thot!" she spat with an attitude.

Ignoring her ass, I pressed play on *True To The Game*. I thought about a compromise but my patience with Nya, especially high, was nonexistent, plus I was in here first. She better shut up and watch this movie. Surprisingly, she did just that. She rolled another blunt, and we smoked and watched the movie. After the pizza and cookies were done, we smashed that shit. I was full and loaded by the end of the movie and fell right to sleep.

I WOKE up at three in the afternoon the next day, and it was quiet as hell, which meant Luca and Diamond still hadn't made it home yet. Going upstairs to pee and check on the girls, I got up and headed upstairs. There was a note on the bedroom door where the girls had slept from Nya.

*Say, I took the girls out for brunch they chilling with me today get yourself situated then hit me up, sister. We're going on a date.*

*~Nya*

I smiled reading the letter that Nya left me. This is why I love my sister. She really considers me, and I can certainly appreciate that.

Proceeding to the bathroom, I handled my business, started the shower putting it as hot as it could go and went into the bedroom to pick out what I was going to be wearing today. Deciding on a cute white t-shirt dress with a deep V neckline with *Unbreakable* scrolled in hot pink lettering that I got from Forever 21, I was content with the outfit knowing that it was going to go perfect with the hot pink clear Nike's Dime let me have since her feet had swelled up.

Dime was really going through the motions with this pregnancy. On top of that, the hoe Hazel has been doing all she could to be relevant when she knows damn well she was not it. My brother's been done with her, and I just found it funny how she keeps playing this role like she still had it like that. All I know is the way she keeps trying Dime is some other shit, and sis is itching to beat that ass pregnant and all. My brother's not gone let that shit go down though. Hopefully, the bitch catches a hint before Rayna gets in town. She was already on that kick to beat Hazel's ass from the last encounter Dime told her about.

Hazel had better be cool while Rae's here. She's coming to town in two weeks for some poetry stuff she's got going on. Rayna is so talented, and I wanted to reach out to her. Nobody knows that I secretly write stories except Nya. I'm not no Rayna Rain, the poet, but I got a few little poems that I was thinking about putting in my stories. They were mostly about becoming a teen mother and the bullshit with Amod.

Getting in the shower, I let the water pour all over me soaking up my long nappy hair. It was stretched yesterday and a little bit ago, but now with the water pouring over my strands, my hair shriveled up close to my scalp. I saturated my hair with the natural Shea butter shampoo that my mother got from the African website shop. After rinsing my hair, I washed my body with the strawberry tropical Olay body wash. I kept thinking about the situation with Amod. He has my car again. Luckily, my mother and father are loving on each other so much that they haven't been on my case about the bullshit with Mod, and I was grateful.

Washing up a couple more times, I finally rinsed off and wrapped the big black towel around my body. I love this mansion. It was everything, and knowing my brother, it will definitely be passed down for generations. I am so happy about the new beauty entering the family. Alani is about to have a cousin, and you couldn't tell her anything! She literally wants to use my phone daily to check on her "Sparkly" and baby cousin. I adored my baby girl. I am still amazed at the growth of her little personality, which, in my opinion, is the most rewarding part about having a child. I swear watching baby girl grow is by far my favorite thing about motherhood.

Standing in the mirror, I wiped the fog off and opened the door to let the steam out. I brushed my teeth and then searched through the hair products that Dime kept under the sink. Rayna stayed sending shit for Diamond to try for her hair. She just recently told me she would send me some natural hair products as well. Grabbing the Echo olive oil styling gel, Murray, edge control, and coconut milk spray, I moved on to detangling my hair. Once finished, I section my hair in order to do a smooth, sleek bun to the back with a deep part. My curls are too tight not to have the waves, so once I was satisfied with the bun, I wrapped a gray bandana around my hair so that it will lie down.

Heading into the bedroom, I laid across the bed and looked through my phone. I decided to call Amod's stupid ass again since I wanted my car back, but he didn't pick up. *Typical.* It was now four in the afternoon, so where this boy was at, I couldn't tell you. Dismissing the thought altogether, I called my sister. Placing her on speaker, I grabbed the hot pink nail polish and began to paint my natural nails.

"You ready?" she said, picking up the phone.

"Yeah, where you at?"

"Don't worry about it, Keith," she said, impersonating Nivea, the singer in the old classic "Laundromat" song. Playing right along with her goofy self, I responded to her.

*"You mocking me? Sound like you mocking me."*

*"Don't nobody gotta mock you?"*

*"Yeah, you mocking me. You get your little record deal and think you all that."*

We both started blurting out the beginning lyrics.

*"You's a lying cheating son of a!"* Before we busted out laughing.

"I'm on my way to you now. Are you ready yet?" she questioned.

"By the time you get here, I will be."

"Luna, don't have me waiting on you son!"

"Byeee, Keith!" I clicked on her ass.

After letting my nails dry by blowing on them and using the mini fan, I got up to finish my hair and put my lashes on. I decided on a deep black lip and proceeded to do my brows. I was feeling myself as I removed the bandana. Loving my waves, I finished my hair by grabbing the hair toothbrush and slicking my edges with the edge control. Looking through the jewelry box I keep over here, I decided on a silver choker necklace and diamond stud earrings.

Cleaning up my mess, I headed back in the room and got dressed, putting on a pink bra and panty set from Lane Bryant. The t-shirt dress was a tad shorter then I was comfortable with showcasing my thick thighs, so I decided to put some black spandex shorts underneath to feel more confident in the fit. Afterwards, I packed my pink over the shoulder purse with the lipstick I was wearing, my charger, phone, and wallet. Putting on ankle socks, I put the pink Nikes on and headed downstairs to wait on my sister.

I love going on dates with my twin. When we were younger, my mom and dad used to take turns going on dates with us. It wasn't too often that we all four went together, and I can't say why. All I know is as we grew older it just became my and Nya's thing to take each other on a date, spend some sister time, and really soak up how wonderful we are, which is what our parents would tell us every time we went on a date with one of them. Cleaning up our mess from last night as I waited, Nya had perfect timing because as soon as I finished, she was honking like crazy. *She is gone alarm these white people with her childish ass.*

Heading out to her new Lexus that she convinced my dad to buy her last week due to the good ass grades, she finished her summer courses with and her car continuously breaking down. I hopped in the car and put my seatbelt on. My mom was big mad about this new ride since she is adamant about us doing what we are supposed to do without expecting rewards for what we just need to be doing— her words— luckily, Nya shut her ass up knowing the car would be a sexy ass memory if she got out of pocket.

This ride was everything. It was silver sleek and dope as hell. I felt myself getting jealous, but at the same time, she deserved it. She really goes hard in school.

"Roll this up," Nya said, handing me a bag of weed and a gar.

I wasn't smoking today, but I'll roll her blunt. I can really pearl. We used to smoke heavily as teenagers, but I slowed up once I had Lani since my ass be tweaking, and I was scared as hell about messing some shit up as a new mom.

She drove to the daiquiri shop. I knew the route and her routine.

"Where are the girls?" I asked, missing my baby and surprised that I didn't get a phone call from her today. I'm so attached to Alani, so I'm not even gone stunt like I'm not kind of salty that she didn't call me.

"With Zeriah and Kyrie."

"Awe, that's why she ain't call me, Lani is so fake," I joked.

She loved her big cousin, and Zeriah loved her back. Their bond was hella cute. Although I'm hating cuz she doesn't know anybody now. I love how involved he is with my love bug. It's been like that since I had her. Everybody adored Alani. I seriously felt the judgment in high school with my big belly, struggling to all my classes, but my family never treated me like an outcast. The support was so real.

After I did my shit pearling the blunt, I snapped a picture with the caption *"Get you a wife that can cook and pearl your blunts."* I then posted it on my Snapchat. After handing the blunt to Nya, I turned the music up and started a Snap video as Nya drove cheifin' on her blunt. Drizzy Drake was playing my new favorite song, "Mob Ties". Hell, Nya is so obsessed with the man! He is dope, but she is extra. Go in her bedroom or dorm, and it's a Drake movement in that hoe! I was spitting the lyrics and felt that shit in my soul.

*"I'm sick of these niggas*
*Sick of these niggas*
*Hire some help, get rid of these niggas*
*Fuck what it was, it is what it is*
*Whatever you did, it is what it is."*

I NEEDED this drink I'm sick of this shit. I called Amod again about my car, and the nigga igged my calls again. I swear I'm trying my best not to get on bullshit since I'm not the petty twin, but Lord knows I'll let Zeriah beat Mod's disrespectful ass. I love him so much, but he got me fucked up, taking advantage of my kindness, and where the hell is this nigga car at? I swear to God that if my parents cuss me out again behind him, I'm sending Riah at him. I don't care anymore.

Pulling up at the daiquiri shop, I cleared my head and just was ready to date my sister. She looked pretty as hell with her glossy, purple-tinted lips, lashes, and long locs pulled to the side and falling over her right eye. She was beautiful. Her swag was official as well she had on black biker shorts with a purple checkered shirt wrapped around her waist and black halter that covered her little titties down her stomach and stopping above her belly button. We had on the same shoes except hers were purple. I guess our twin telepathy was on point today. She had silver hoops in her ears and a silver Pandora charm bracelet that Lu had got her, another gift for them straight A's she ended her summer courses with. She deserved a good time and all the gifts.

Hopping out the car, I wanted a Hurricane with four shots of vodka, so that's exactly what I ordered. Nya got the special. We were regulars at the daiquiri shop. We were underage, but my girl Trendy worked here, and she always hooked us up. She used to work at my job until she popped my supervisor Karen in the mouth for talking racist. No lie, I be at work counting to ten. She's out of control with it, and it was an ongoing struggle for my girl to let it ride, but hell, that day Trendy wasn't for none! She was ready to get fired, and she did! I missed my work friend. I didn't realize how much until now.

"What's been up, Luna? You still dealing with Karen's bullshit?" she asked me.

"Girllll, fuck Karen. I need my coins! I need cheese for my egg like Cardi said."

"I hear you, shawty."

"What you been up to?"

"Working and minding my business and ready to bust August in his big ass head if he keeps playing with me." I laughed. Trendy and August has some crazy shit going, but hell, they love the hell out of one another, and it was evident, even when they cutting up, and they definitely be cutting the fuck up.

"Aiight my girl, I'm going to keep in touch, so hit my line. I'm about to beat Nya's ass on this pool table." I passed on my number, and she agreed to do just that.

Grabbing my drink, I walked over to the pool table where Nya was racking the balls. We played the game, and I busted her ass like always. She really sucked at pool, but you can't tell Nya to give up on shit, so that's why I knew we were always coming here to get a buzz and for her to try her best to beat me in pool. So, of course, I talked my shit about my win. I was good and drunk. We were going to get food next.

Leaving out with Nya behind me, I saw my car. I thought I might be tripping, so I went closer. Something told me I wasn't though, so I was focused on my car. My heart rate sped up, and I felt my pressure rising. I walked up to that bitch on the passenger side and seen Mod eating a bitch's pussy. My heart sank to my stomach, and before I knew it, I snatched the passenger door open and started fucking Mod up in mid-lick.

Realizing that he was getting fucked up, he tried his best to get away from me. I mean that nigga was really trying to get away, but I was on that ass, and we tumbled out the driver's side door on to the parking lot ground. I kept fucking him up. I didn't give a fuck as I sat on that nigga punching him, and I dared his random pussy-eating ass to huff on me with his trifling ass. It was official I was sending my brother and cousins for his hat!

Trendy and security came out, and as security snatched me up, I peeped Trendy kick the hell out of Mod. *Oh, she's a real one.* Looking around, I saw security snatch Nya off the bitch Mod was with. Nya just wanted action. I was unconcerned with that bitch. Ain't no telling if she knew or not, but hell, I can't control Nya's ass, so the hoe was at the wrong place wrong time— issaaa casualty!

I ran back up on Mod since the guard had slacked up eyeing Nya. After busting that nigga in his eye one last time, I snatched my keys off the ground that must have fallen out my ride or off this nigga, but I now had possession of my damn keys.

"Shawty, chill mane, just chill."

"BITCH! DONT TALK TO ME WITH THAT HOE'S PUSSY ON YOUR TONGUE!" I was 1800 hot jumping up and down. For me not to be trying to watch *Friday* last night, I sure felt like Pinky when he thought Craig was stealing.

*"SAY. ANOTHER. MUTHAFUCKING WORD. SAY SOMETHING ELSE, AND THIS SHIT IS OVER, AND I AIN'T PLAYING, NIGGA!"* I

thought, hearing the voice of Pinky blaring in my head from the movie.

I was so pissed off and hurt that tears poured down my cheeks. As soon as Nya saw the tears, she rushed the bitch again. Any other day I'll tell my sister to chill since this bitch wasn't the problem, nor did she disrespect me. Hell, for all we knew, she was just trying to get her nut, and I ain't no lame ass pressed bitch. I can respect that, but my feelings were hurt, and security wasn't letting up. I wanted to fuck Amod up some more over my hurt feelings. Over this shit, I told security that I was good. They gave me a little space, but not much because Amod was still looking like he wanted to talk or some shit. I was not playing with him. He better shut his ass up and get the fuck on.

I hit the locks on my car, Nya closed the doors, and we headed to her Lexus. Hopping in her ride, I spaced out I felt like the goofiest bitch ever but only because this nigga disrespected the hell out of me. However, I knew I still had to build a bridge and get the hell over it for Alani's sake. As we drove home, my mind was gone as we headed to the house. Pulling up, we got a call that Dime had gone into labor.

# 8

## MARS

I t wasn't an option for a nigga not to be great. I've been grinding and I ain't gone lie, I've been stalking Little's ass for the last couple weeks. She was acting like she wasn't trying to fuck with me anymore. I was feeling fucked up missing her. She fell all the way back on a nigga. I'm sure she put my ass on do not disturb or some shit since I couldn't get in contact with that ass. Deciding to try my luck and stop by Luca's crib, I knew she was over there since I stopped at her parents' house first. Her mom told me they are having a celebration for her over there. Before pulling up, I went to get her a few gifts.

Pulling up at Luca's house, shit was live as hell. I decided to bring one gift inside knowing that she was most likely gone be on her bullshit. After I parked my car and hopped out, I headed to the door to knock. Once inside, I greeted Luna and looked around low key trying to see where Little was at. Peeping her in the back, I headed her way. She was fine as fuck in a white skirt and yellow bikini. Her locs were in a ponytail on top of her head, and she had shades on her face.

Walking towards her, she tried to walk past a nigga, but I grabbed her ass up. I wasn't having it. I missed her. Ana was acting like a bitch. She was being sneaky and moving fucking suspicious. It's all good though. Her ass was about to be fucking out of luck if I found out she was on some foul shit.

I heard Dime had a false alarm. They thought she was dropping the baby, but it wasn't time. She looked hot and mean as hell sitting on the lounge chair, getting her feet rubbed by Luca. It was now the end of August, and she was due soon. That nigga Lu seemed beyond ready for her to drop that fucking baby.

"Mars, move from around me."

"I just wanted to congratulate you on you passing all your classes and shit, Little." I handed her a gift.

"I'm good. I don't want shit from you give it to your bitch." That's cute, Little, you jealous.

"You are my little bitch," I said, and the drink she had went flying at my face, liquor, and the red plastic cup.

I snatched her ass up and dragged her somewhere more secluded. Her ass was showing out, and a nigga ain't have time for that shit. I wasn't in the mood. We ducked off downstairs away from everybody else. I wiped my face with a paper towel. She was cussing my ass out, but I tuned her out she love a nigga, and I love her ass back. All that rowdy shit baby is on is uncalled for.

I bent her ass over knowing what the problem is. She missed this dick and a nigga putting pressure on that pussy, so I did just that after I removed her skirt and bikini bottoms eating her pussy from the back. This will forever be my pussy. She hurt a nigga with that petty shit. That's why I didn't want to bring it there with her. Mane, if she does that shit again, ain't no telling if shit gone go as smooth. Out of respect for Luca and the fact that I wasn't supposed to be fucking her young ass anyway, I let her make it. Allowing that shit be what it was, I cut her ass off. I was about to bless her with this dick since I needed Little to get her attitude together and quickly. Her ignoring a nigga and shit just wasn't feeling right.

"Mmmm mmmm, fuck, I missed you."

"Shut up," I said, picking her up and sucking on her small ass titties.

Lifting her, I had a seat on the couch and put her pussy in my face. I started feasting on that shit. I was craving her sweet pussy. She called herself being over a nigga, but I knew that shit was short lived. I treated her ass the way I treated her because a nigga holds grudges. Yeah, I told her ass, we were just having fun, and she wasn't my girl, but that shit didn't mean she could fuck with other niggas, and her ass knew it too. She was being spiteful, and even at nineteen, I knew a spiteful bitch wasn't the headache I needed. That petty shit will have both of us dead. Although I respected Luca and Bear, I wasn't scared of them niggas. If I'm wrong, I'm wrong, but ain't no nigga gone have me on my knees like I'm his bitch. So if he wasn't gone be cool with me killing his fine, petty ass sister, I had to let her ass go.

I was ready to slide into this pussy, so I rubbed the tip on her clit. I tried to slide into her, but she was tight as hell. What the fuck? I was struggling to get in. A nigga was sweating and all. I only had the tip in and was ready to bust. She was moaning and doing a sexy little whine, making me brick up harder. I reached around her and played with her clit.

"It's okay, shawty. Let me get this pussy, mami, relax."

I was biting my lip, trying not to go out like a little boy I couldn't believe I left this alone. She was tightening up, so I spread her cheeks, pushing them apart to spread that pussy a little more. Mane, once a nigga did that, she was creaming on my shit, and that pussy was gripping my dick. Watching her beautiful sex faces, I started talking to her.

"You missed this dick shawty," I said, groaning.

"Marsssss!"

"It's pressure huh, Little?" I questioned, giving her deep strokes grinding in her wet pussy that was gripping and coating my dick with her cum. Ohh shit, I had the ugly screw face on trying to hold my nut. I swear a nigga could live in this pussy.

"Mmmhmmm... PRESSSUREEE! Please, don't stop! Please, I'm about to cumm, oh my gosh!" she screamed out as she drowned my dick with her juices.

She was whining and shit, and it was just turning a nigga on more, so I started swerving in her shit. Hitting against them walls a couple of strokes later, she drenched my dick again. That pussy gripped my dick tight as fuck. It had a vice grip! *Word? Little's coochie*, I though as I held back my nut.

I shook my head up and down. This pussy was on another level. This was probably why I stopped fucking. I knew a nigga was gone be out here bad and murdering shit. I slapped her on the ass again since she was gripping my shit. She was trembling. The first time I fucked at nineteen flashed in my head as I groaned and emptied my seeds inside her. Flipping her over onto her back, I tongued her down, sucking on her bottom lip. Looking in her eyes, they were glossy as hell, and she looked drained.

Hearing commotion, we redressed and headed upstairs quickly, trying to see what the hell was going on. When we went upstairs, that nigga Riah was beating the fuck out of Cole, and Kamoni was crying her eyes out. Lunya looked way too calm for all the bullshit going down at her celebration. I had that ass on a dick high, so she was unbothered. The crazy shit about the whole thing for me was where all these muthafuckas came from. I knew we weren't fucking that long. Everybody was letting Cole get his ass beat while Kamoni cried hysterically. She sat her ass right on one of the lounge chairs off to the side, not moving. Her sister looked like she dared her to get her ass up. I was confused as to what Rayna, Bear, Drip, and that nigga Heavy Drip's number one overseer to his side operation was doing here. It was also a pretty brown skin female with auburn hair that I never saw before who sat skimming her phone.

I tried to intervene since Cole was my nigga, but as I walked up, everybody eyes pinned me, and at least three muthafuckas looked like they would fuck me up. Hell, the Mora chick even aimed her piece at a nigga. I was confused as fuck, and Lunya's ass was making two plates like she was Ray Charles to the bullshit. She sat down at the table, and Luca passed her a blunt as everybody watched that nigga Cole get his ass beat or just continued doing shit like Riah wasn't fucking this nigga up. I mean he was beating the nigga like he spat on his mama and snatched the nigga's chain.

"Say, baby, you want a crawfish boudin?" Nya asked me

distracting my ass temporarily since a nigga was hungrier den a bitch after that workout.

"Shut yo ass up, Kamoni Amora Gains! You shouldn't have brought this clown ass nigga here in the first place! The fuck!" Kamora screamed at her, and Moni covered her face with her hands, smothering her cries as she shook from crying so hard.

That nigga Bear looked like a proud big ass don with his shades on and a handful of Rayna's ass in his hands, kissing on her neck as he watched his little brother fuck Cole up. I was trying to see how long they were gone let this shit go down. Diamond, Luna, and Kyrie came from the back, and Diamond walked up to Drip and Heavy with her big ass stomach leading the way.

"Yawl can Cash App me my funds," Dime said further confusing the fuck out of me. Bro, what the entire fuck?

"Nah little bitch, I want my shit in cash," Bear said, slapping Rayna's ass. She laughed and kissed his lips.

"Mann, that nigga can come back," Heavy said. This psycho ass nigga was tripping Riah was dead ass gone kill this nigga over a bet and was everybody in on the shit?

# 9

# DIAMOND "DIME" MASON

I was one miserable pregnant bitch. I couldn't decide if I wanted to suck Luca's dick or cut it off. This little girl had my ass going through the motions. I couldn't keep my shit together, and I know Luca was sick of my shit because I was sick of me. I was pissed off. What the entire fuck was Lula Rayari Wright doing inside of me? She was getting popped when she finally brought her little ass into the world, playing with my emotions and shit— literally. I just knew she was coming two weeks ago, but NOPE. I'm still pregnant and emotional as fuck.

Rayna had been here since the false alarm refusing to leave until this stubborn ass daughter of mine come since she thought she missed it. No lie, I'd been having fun living with my bestie for the last two weeks. She had been back and forth from here and Baton Rouge since she been getting to know the new artist for an upcoming event. That's where she and Bear were right now. She was coming back later today for Nya's celebration.

I was so proud of my girl for pulling through them summer cour-ses. That shit is not easy at all. My ass wasn't about to be taking no summer courses. I was happy as fuck to go back to school after I finally dropped Lula though. I wanted my damn body back, and every time I looked at the dark ass line going down my stomach, I got sad. That shit was ugly as hell. I'm not even worried about Lula coming out weird looking anymore, and I told her that already, so why her little ass was just chilling at the bottom of my stomach doing flips and kicking on me at three in the morning waking me up and pissing me off daily, I didn't know. I had been evicted this little girl out my womb.

I was walking my fat ass up and down the stairs huffing and puffing when Luca came in with all the food his mom cooked for today. He started to say some shit but shut his ass up because he knows my ass would start crying. I wanted this baby out. I felt ugly, my feet were swollen, my nose had spread, and Rae called me Miss Piggy yesterday. Plus, that bitch Hazel kept trying me, but she was getting a *real* eviction since she thought shit was sweet and she had it like that. Hazel left a Rolex on Luca's desk at the restaurant not knowing he sent me in since I took over managing his books since Ajinne stayed going back and forth. She went to New York a few weeks ago with her husband Bishop to see her brother Kingston. I liked Ajinne, but this bitch Hazel had to go, and I was dead serious. She got one more time to call my man about that condo that he allowed her to stay in. I can't believe Hazel had really left a gift, talking about it's an appreciation present. She knocked on the office door thinking she was gone see my man but got me.

Mr. Wright saved her ass because with my emotion running away from baby Lula and prolonging her stay in my body, I was beyond homicidal. So, when this bitch knocked on *our* office door and waltzed her thirsty ass in without a response with big ass smile on her face looking all slim while I am frustrated and round, I couldn't help chucking the jewelry box at that hoe, cracking her stupid as in the head. My big ass couldn't make it around the mahogany desk quick enough, so I snatched the cup filled with pens, chucking them at her ass too. I was fed up with this hoe dehydrated ass antics. Clearly, the warning Luca gave her when I popped up wasn't moving the bitch. I was DONE, fucking DONE. I swear if Mr. Wright didn't come in when he did, I was gone give the ass whooping she'd been begging me for.

This hoe was hard up, like who raised this bitch? As I went to tag that ass, Mr. Wright was right on time with the rescue a pressed bitch foundation. That spiked my pressure up, and that's what caused the false alarm labor. I was rushing Lula. She had baked long enough. Fuck whatever due date they gave. Hell, they don't know anything.

"Ma, I got you a red bean plate to eat right now if you're hungry," Luca said sweetly. However, my crazy emotional ass heard, *"I got your fat ass a plate. I know you hungry."*

"So I just got to want to eat because I'm fat forreaaaal, Luca? I don't want no red bean plate. I'm on a fucking diet, and you know that!" I screamed at him and burst out in tears.

Looking stressed out, Luca walked up to me. He wiped my tears from my face with his palms and kissed me softly. He did it repeatedly until I started kissing him back passionately. Luca picked me up and carried me upstairs, ran me a hot bath, and stripped me out my clothes. I was about to say something, but he shook his head "no" and kissed my lips, clearing my mind. Hitting the sound speaker in our bathroom, he stripped out of his clothes as well and joined me in the tub. It was ironic as hell that Ed Sheeran's "Thinking Out Loud" came on and it was hella perfect.

As Luca washed my body, he sang along with the lyrics, and I felt each verse in each caress as he spread soap all over my body wiping away the sweat that covered my skin from me walking up and down the stairs trying to get Lula out of me.

*"I'm thinking 'bout how people fall in love in mysterious ways*
*Maybe just the touch of a hand*
*Oh me I fall in love with you every single day."*

HE WAS gentle as he washed us up, and I was getting turned on, which led to my big ass bent over the tub with a bath pillow cushioning my stomach getting dicked down by my future husband. He had to be slow with the strokes to make sure he didn't hurt me. My ass was enjoying this dick so much that happy tears gathered in my eyes. After I came, I washed myself up one final time and rinsed off. Luca got out and scooped me up in a towel. Drying me off, he grabbed the raw Shea and cocoa butter that is supposed to clear up this ugly ass line and stretch marks. He rubbed it all over my body, making me feel like a brand new person. Luca traveled down my body and ate my pussy until I came in his mouth twice. I was done for. I was floating off as I felt a big ass t-shirt that smelled like the love of my life wrap around my body. The soft comforter was the end for me a drifted off to sleep.

## 10

# LUCA WRIGHT

After putting Diamond to sleep, I headed to smoke and get ready to get shit started for Nya's celebration. When my lady's not right, I'm not right. I had the papers served to Hazel this morning. The bitch done eat up all the help a nigga had for her ass. She is stressing my lady, which means she is stressing my fucking daughter out. A nigga is not even gone lie. I was praying every day for my baby girl to bring her slow ass on. All this crying shit Dime's been on since she got pregnant was some frustrating ass shit. There was no point of even talking to her. She was crying regardless.

I let the situation with Hazel draw itself out. With Bear's annoying ass in my ear since he was at the end of the road trying to stop Rae from popping up on Hazel and *"dragging the bitch for playing with her sister because she pregnant"*, I knew I had to move fast before the RAIN poured down on ME and Hazel's bitch ass. With them two talking they shit, my lady crying about the stupidest shit, add the twins and lastly my pops, Hazel was done with, and Rae had no issue letting me know. *"That's your EX! Act like you know that shit before I go to jail! Get your nuts you acting like a whole bitch out here!"* she spat at me when she had to rush to the hospital for the false alarm labor.

Knowing Rayna's rude ass was right, I got right on the shit quickly.

I felt bad that Hazel couldn't just be cool and get her shit right with the help I was providing, but fuck it now. That's all on that bitch's body. She didn't give a fuck, so why should I?

I focused on setting the house up for Nya. I was proud of my baby sister. After shit was situated, I went into the kitchen and started getting all the food together. My queen did her shit, and everything smelled good as shit. Per usual we had all of Nya's favorites— chicken, boudin, tacos, gumbo, king cake, and more.

Looking at the time, it was about that time to start everything. Nya, Luna, and Kyrie had come in here a few minutes ago. Riah was already here since he'd been staying with me over the summer so that we can do training in the mornings. Today is about Nya. We were having a pool party for her. We were going to be playing spades, bones, and just having a good ass time to celebrate my sister success.

My wife was in better spirits after her nap. She had got dressed in a baby pink sundress, showcasing my daughter. She had on furry white slides, and her hair that had grown past her shoulders was pulled on top of her head in a ponytail. My wife was sexy as fuck. My baby girl had her feeling insecure, but shit, her carrying my child just made her hotter in my eyes.

I had taken her slides off to rub her swollen ass feet. She ain't make it no better being on her shit all the time, and she was doing the most Googling shit to go in labor. My daughter wasn't due until the fifth of September, so why she couldn't chill and leave my baby alone was beyond a nigga. I ain't gone lie though I was sick of her ass waking me up at three in the morning in tears talking shit about my baby and her back hurting. Hell, I felt like Lula's little ass was already here since I had to feed Dime and rub her back and stomach for her to take her crybaby ass back to sleep. I wanted our daughter name to be Luciana or Diamond Jr., but since we did the hat pull method, Lula won. We already discussed that our daughter middle name would be after Rae, so Rayari is what we came up with. I rubbed Dime feet then leaned over to kiss Lula who was supposed to be making her way into the world in two weeks.

"Say, daughter, mommy wants her body back, and daddy wants to meet you, my baby. When you trying to come through?" I placed my hand on her stomach, and baby girl was kicking up a storm instantly making a nigga smile.

I see Mars come in, and he immediately went to talk to Nya. They asses needed to get it together, but of course, I was minding my business on that shit. He was a good dude at his core, and if he fucked over my sister, she knew how I was coming behind her ass and so did he! In the meantime, I'm gone stay out they shit unless I feel I need to do otherwise. I trusted my sister to make her own decisions, especially with her love life.

Dime and I watched the exchange of words between they ass before the red plastic cup and whatever was in it that Nya was holding went flying at that nigga. He snatched her up, and they ducked off. I just shook my head and kissed my wife. Luna has come to where we were with Bear, Rayna, Drip, Heavy and a new server at the Lounge in Baton Rouge. Her name is Earth. She was quiet, but she was a hard worker, and now she was going to Atlanta with Rayna, aka Rainy or Rayna Rain the poet.

Rayna's last event gave her so much support that she had come up with the poet name Rainy. She also collaborated with a beautiful black woman who owned a couple of all-black art galleries right here in Louisiana, NOLA and Baton Rouge, plus one in Atlanta. That shit was amazing. *"For us by us"* were her words. I was trying to throw some wine tasting events in that bitch soon. The gallery was on some other level shit, showcasing some of the great paintings of black history hidden from so many black people, so I was gone be hitting up Mrs. Kristen KAWD Downing soon. Hell, I wanted to dedicate a whole room in my big ass home to my love and black women. I'm gone have Rayna plug me in don't worry about it.

"Wassam, bih?" Bear said as he sat at the table that I had set up for a spades game.

We had the Bluetooth playing. It was still early, so nobody was really here yet. Riah and Kyrie were ducked off on the basketball court on the other side of the pool. Dime, Rayna, Luna, and Earth had gone in the kitchen, so it was just the guys. Bear started rolling up, and Drip was shuffling the cards.

"Who wants to get fucked up in these spades?" Drip asked. I wasn't no card player I'll fuck them up in some Dominoes in a few though.

"I'm down, bitch. Let me go get my partners!" that nigga Bear said hopping up, confusing the fuck out of Heavy and Drip. I just started laughing since I already know how this nigga does when he is playing.

"Did that nigga say partners as in more than one? What the fuck?" Heavy said, sitting across from Drip.

"Yeah Jose, nigga I said partners," Bear's racist ass said since Heavy is Hispanic. He was holding Rayna's hand with Luna right behind him.

"Nigga, my name is Christian or Heavy, the fuck?" He mugged the shit out of Bear.

"Whatever C, that shit is irrelevant. Are yawl trying to get this ass whooping or what?" Bear disrespectful ass said dismissively, causing me to shake my head.

Heavy mugged that nigga, but you could see him letting the shit go, clearly this wasn't his first encounter with Bear. He just shook his head.

"Aiight, my partners ready let's go," Bear said, sitting down and pulling Rae on his lap as Luna sat across from them.

"Nigga, are you serious?" Drip asked, laughing.

"Bitch, let my partner cut them cards so that me and my other partner can get our hand!"

I shook my head. I'm sure this nigga is cheating by adding a partner, but shit, Luna's been that nigga's spade partner since she was ten. He taught her how to play. Bear played against Rae a few times, and she's a beast. She busted his ass all four time, so he just added her as his partner since she and Dime are the only ones other than my parents who can beat him and Luna.

"Whatever bitch, all three of yawl bout to take this L, so I ain't tripping," Heavy said boasting as Luna cut the cards, and Drip started passing them out.

Passing the blunt around the table, I went to get some more weed and gars from upstairs. On my way there, I stopped in the kitchen and Earth, Dime, and now Kamora was in there. I didn't know when her ass got here, but I hugged her and asked about her grandmother, who was a warrior after all the shit she's been through. That's Mora story to tell though. Her ass wasn't no slouch either. I kissed Dime and headed upstairs. Looking for my shit, I couldn't find it where I put it. I knew I had some up here, but I knew for sure that I had some shit downstairs.

Dime came in the room and asked me what I was looking for.

"I think I put it in here when I was cleaning up, and you don't want to go downstairs baeee. Nya's getting booty," she said getting my shit from a drawer that I didn't look in and giving me a goofy ass smile.

"She wants me to fuck her up, and your ass could have kept that shit to yourself," I told her childish ass, pinning her to the door and kissing her on the neck.

"She a grown ass wo—"

I cut her off. I ain't wanna hear that shit. Grown or not, that's my baby sister. I wasn't gone discuss or think of her getting booty. Hell, matter fact, I don't want to believe neither one of the twins were fucking. Luna had a whole baby, and a nigga was still in denial. Lunya is out of line fucking in my crib.

Clearing my head of that shit, I kissed down Dime's body to taste my pussy.

Removing her panties, I picked her up and laid her on her back on the bed and licked up her slit before diving my tongue all in. As I was going dumb and focused on making my lady cum, we heard hella commotion going downstairs. My ass wasn't done yet though. I didn't get me earlier, so I was about to get me now.

"Bbbbbbabyyy, we need to go cccheck on our houseeeee ohhh!" she said as I slid inside her. *Mane, fuck all that. After I bust my nut, we gone check,* I thought as I continued to stroke her fire ass pussy.

# 11

## KYRIE

"**N**igga, you're not gone beat me. Give it up!" Riah's annoying ass said with a light sweat while I was soaking in that shit.

I was really trying to get a win, but he was too next level for my ass. I was tired as fuck.

"Good game though little bitch," he said, walking off and I followed him since I needed to get my change of clothes from my car.

Wiping the sweat from my forehead with the bottom of my shirt, we stopped at the spades table where Luna was she looked sexy as fuck with Bantu knots and a red one-piece swimsuit, shorts, and slides on. I was eyeing her with lust. We made eye contact staring at one another. Mane, I wanted shawty in the best way. I felt my dick bricking up I swear if sh...

"Ayee, little bitch!" that nigga Bear said, hitting the table. "Get away from the damn table distracting my partner. Heyy Lulu, focus," he said, snapping his fingers at her and pointing at him and his lady that was on his lap, and then the middle of the table where the cards was sliding. We all couldn't help but laugh. He was serious about this game.

"My bad, cuz," she said, smiling and redirecting her attention back to the cards.

Deciding to get up with her later, I went to get my clothes bag from my car and headed back inside to one of the bathrooms. I showered and changed into some cargo tan shorts and a blue polo shirt before going downstairs. I saw Dime coming upstairs as I went down, and she asked me if I was good. I told her I was straight and continued on my way.

Riah was sitting down on the couch in the living room now dressed in black cargo shorts with a Nike tank top rolling a blunt. I scrolled my phone seeing that I had a missed call from my little fuck buddy, Claya. I made plans to slide on her after I left here. We went back to where everyone was in the back, and Kamoni was arguing with Kamora about that nigga Cole.

"Mora, I just want to drop off a gift for Nya, that's it. Damn, we about to go!" Moni yelled.

"How you gone try to drop off a gift and bring this lame ass nigga to your bestie's celebration after the shit you was on, and who the fuckkkkk you yelling at, my girl?" Mora asked in an icy ass voice about to walk up, but some Hispanic dude lazily held her back by the strap of the purse around her body. He was one hell of a multitasker since he managed to hold his cards, hold Mora at bay, and play his card on the spades table when it was his turn.

"Say, yawl distracting us with all that we trying to get this win," Bear said nonchalantly.

"Bitch, we up!" the Hispanic said as his partner scooped up a book.

"Mane fuck outta here, Jose. This is our game, my nigga."

"Nigga my fucking name is Heavy!" he spat looking like he would take it to the streets behind his name. Bear was a solid ass nigga, but this swole ass Hispanic didn't seem worried at all.

"Mane, Moni, fuck all these weak ass people, we out. I told your dumb ass not to even come over here in the first place, fuck you pressed for friends for? Let's get the fuck before I slap the fuck out this bitch for steady disrespecting you and me," Cole ass said, mugging Kamora getting the entire table attention.

Zeriah put his blunt out. Mora was his people off the strength that he and Moni had some shit going when they were younger. Add in the fact that Cole had Kamoni, and he felt like she was his. My boy was about to get on his bullshit, and I was gone let him do his shit.

"Nigga, try that shit little boy, you got the right bitch. I ain't the one or the fucking two. You're out yo lane little bitch, and Moni's not going no muthafucking where so now what?"

Mora bucked at that nigga, but the Hispanic nigga whose name I now knew was Heavy was still holding her back. With the way he was looking at Cole now, it was gone be some shit if he blew hot air at Mora.

"BITCH WHAT?"

"She said what she said, ugly ass dude. She ain't stutter or nothing!" the dark skin short chick said that was sitting on Bear's lap.

"Mane, fuck this shit. Let's go, Moni!" Cole screamed, but as Kamora glared at her little sister, Moni hesitated, pissing this nigga off further.

He gritted his teeth. "BITCH, I SAID, LET'S GO!"

She jumped, and tears rushed to her eyes sliding down her cheeks, but she still barely moved. He went to snatch on her, but Riah cracked his ass with a right hook to the jaw.

"Finally Riah, shit, that nigga was fucking up the vibe. We bout to come back," that nigga Bear said, playing a card.

"Shit, no! Not in this fucking hand," the other nigga that's Heavy partner, said cutting the queen of club with a jack of spade.

"Jump higher next time, baby! He got a partner, and I know yourssss got a fucking club! Not great enough Drip," Luna said, slapping a queen of spade. She was right Heavy had a club, giving the trio the book.

Cole and Riah were going blow for blow as Moni cried and Mora watched Riah beating Cole's ass like a proud mom or some shit. Luca and Dime rushed downstairs. Diamond was walking towards the commotion. I don't know what the fuck she was gone do since she was pregnant as hell, but before she even got close to them niggas, Bear's lady stood up.

"Carmel, itsss cool." They must have had an understanding or some shit since Dime instantly relaxed.

"Ayee, this shit is getting live. I'm gone put some money on the woman beater," the nigga who Luna addressed as Drip said.

"Nigga, you got my brother fucked up. Bet it up," Bear said.

"Double that up. I'm in on this shit. My money's on Riah too" ole girl on Bear's lap said.

"Aiight Rae baby, I'm gone put your money with mine," Bear said all sweet and shit then kissed her lips. That shit was different seeing him actually being respectful. All jokes aside, who knew he had it in him.

"I want to make some money too!" Dime said.

Cole had the upper hand right now since he was bigger in weight, but I wasn't betting against Riah. I knew my nigga wasn't gone let this weak ass boy whoop his ass. I'm not betting no bread though. If you ask me all these muthafuckas are touched in the head to be just acting like they're at a boxing show.

"Aiight, fuck it. I'm with my partna. The woman beater got this shit," Heavy stated.

"Bet," Dime said and sat in the lounge chair that was right in front of them niggas.

She was definitely to close, and I wasn't the only one who felt like that since Luca grabbed one of the arms of the chair and dragged her ass back and to the other side of the spades' table. I know nigga Heavy felt like he spoke too soon. Shit turned for that nigga Cole as Riah rocked his shit and proceeded to give him that work. Diamond must have been hungry because she went into the kitchen and came back with a red bean plate with Luna following behind her.

Fuck it. A nigga's hungry too. I went into the kitchen to see if there were more red beans when Luna came into the kitchen.

"What you looking for?" Luna asked me.

"Some red beans, that shit looked good on Dime's plate."

"My man got that for me. It's rolling too!" Diamond said, entering the kitchen as she went to the refrigerator, grabbing a whole thing of white strawberry cranberry juice.

Shaking my head, I went back outside behind Luna and Dime. Marshad and Lunya had appeared from somewhere. I didn't even know they ass was here. I was wondering why she wasn't at her own celebration. She looked relaxed and happy. Bruh, it was like she couldn't hear or see Riah beating Cole's ass or Kamoni crying hysterically. These people are crazy. Mars tried to get involved, but everybody wanted to get their money, so they mugged his ass. It was personal for Mora, so she didn't hesitate pointing the gun at that nigga Mars, and he stopped dead in his tracks.

The crazies went back in forth on whether or not they should break it up and give Riah the win. It was evident that Cole wasn't coming back from the ass whooping. Riah was currently stomping that nigga, and Heavy still was trying to hold out hoping he wouldn't have to give up the $1500 he put up. It was over with though. Luca told Riah to chill out, but Zeriah was too far gone, so I intervened and got my boy out of there. When I came back, Moni was steady crying.

"Say, I got people on the way here who gone clean that up?" Nya said like that nigga's blood and body was a spill, *crazy muthafucka*.

"I called the people already. They're on the way now to come get him. Don't worry," Luna said then slammed down a big joker over the little joker Heavy put down.

"That's game, bitch!" Bear and his ole lady said in unison, hopping up.

"And yawl set," Luna said, dropping her last two cards that were the ace of spade and queen of a spade. They ass was definitely set because Bear and Rae had the king of spade. Leaning back, she took a sip of her black cherry Mike Hard.

"Who's next?" she questioned, looking dead at me.

I wanted to talk to her. We had been spending time together as friends, and a nigga was feeling her even more. She hadn't been talking too much about Lani's dad, so I didn't know what the fuck she had going on with that nigga, but I would be lying like a muthafucka if I said I cared since my ass only wanted her to have something going on with me fuck that nigga.

"Yawl ass cheated! How are you gone have five players for a four player game anyway, son?"

"Shut yo ass up, Drippten. Yawl wasn't winning regardless," Rae said.

"Mane whatever, Rae Rae, we out this bitch. Be easy yawl!" he said, shaking his head and hugging her before he dapped Bear up and left with Heavy, Mora, and some fine ass chick with auburn hair.

Ignoring all that shit, I focused on Luna's fine ass.

"Come here, shawty."

"What you want, Kyrie?" she said, shuffling the cards.

"That pussy in my mouth, your body in my bed, and this dick in your guts every night for the rest of your fine ass life." Her eyes got big, and she looked around trying to see if anyone heard me. I didn't give no fuck if they did. I was done playing games with her ass.

"Damn, it's like that?" her voice was filled with lust.

"Just like that, come on," I said, pulling her up out the chair. I held her hand and walked out to my car. Once inside my all black Escalade, I pulled off to get some snow cones.

"Where are you taking me? I'm trying to celebrate with my face."

"We're going back shawty, relax," I told her and turned up the music as I drove.

Once we got the snow cones, we parked and walked the streets. She still had her swimsuit on and some shorts with furry slides. We walked, talked, and joked. She was so goofy. I love that shit. We cracked jokes and shared stories about the girls. I was getting to know shawty, and I liked her ass more and more by the second. As we walked back to the car, I was over the games she was playing. I wanted her, so a nigga was gone have her.

"I'm taking you on a date. I know you got shit going with your baby dad, but fuck that nigga." I pinned her ass to the car.

"You telling me or asking me, Mr. Kyrie?"

"Both Mrs. Kyrie." She grinned hard as hell and looked down, showcasing the crispy ass triangle parts that her Bantu knots were in. I lifted her chin kissing her lips.

"What's up?"

"We can go on a date, baby."

"Bet," I said and tongued her fine ass down.

"Let's get back. Nya will get on her bullshit if I miss her celebration," she said pulling away and kissing me back then hopping in my truck.

I hopped in and drove back to Luca and Dime's crib. I had one hand on the wheel, and the other was gripping her thigh as I sped back to the mansion. When we arrived, that bitch was live as fuck. I parked, and we both got out my whip and headed inside. Cole was no longer laying in his blood. Matter fact with all the muthafuckas was in here now having a good ass time. You wouldn't even know that a fight had just taken place in this bitch, not even a good three hours ago.

"I'm about to go find my sister," Luna said trying to walk off, but I pulled her back, tongued kissed her, and gripped her ass before letting her go.

"Now you can go," I said and went to the back where Riah was playing Dominoes with Luca as Dime sat next to him eating boudin and meat pies. No bullshit, her food was looking good as fuck. A nigga was about to get a plate.

Riah was focused on the game while Moni sat on the side of that nigga with the saddest expression looking like Yvette and shit from *Baby Boy*. When she got up, I almost expected that nigga to call out to her like that nigga Jody, but he didn't. He continued to play his game. I took her seat and watched them niggas play. Looking at the score on paper, Luca's ass was up, but Riah had just dominoed, so that put him up getting the points in Luca's hand. I joked with them niggas until Luna came up with a plate of food. She handed it to me and tried to walk off, but I pulled her ass on my lap. This was about to be my lady for sure.

"That's thirty."

"Mane, Luna get the fuck on, he ain't call his money," Riah said, mugging her.

"He was wiping Dime's mouth! Stop trying to cheat, Zeriah Brian," she said, laughing.

"Say, get away from this table, mane," he said, shooing her, but she just ignored his ass.

"Damn, you trying to get this win for real? You ready to cheat! Good looking baby sis, but I was gone call my shit regardless." Luca said.

I was just smashing my food listening to these niggas go back and forth. Nya and Mars had come up.

"Aww, yawl cute!" Nya said and mushed Luna who immediately hopped off my lap to chase after her sister who took off running toward the pool.

"Their asses play all day," Riah said.

"Shit yeah!" Luca co-signed watching Luna try to push Nya in the pool without going in herself, but they both fell in anyway.

"You good, my nigga? My bad I didn't know. Cole had been on some bullshit lately."

"Fuck that, nigga. Hell, you good? Mora was about to pop yo stupid ass. I'm Gucci," Riah said dismissively.

That Gucci shit is lame as hell, but that nigga won't stop saying that cheesy ass shit.

Finishing up my food, I went to throw my plate away and get a drink. As I walked in the kitchen Bear had Rayna bent over the counter giving her dick like this bitch wasn't somewhat packed!

"Aye, little bitch. Get out!"

Did this nigga just kick me out the kitchen at a party? I let that man get him and settled for the water they had outside already. Fuck it. Once I got my drink, I went back to the table where they were still playing bones.

"Say that nigga Bear is getting booty in the kitchen," I said, sitting down.

"Boy, you telling?" Riah said, cracking up. *You fucking right. A nigga wanted a real drink.*

Before I can respond, Luca started talking his shit.

"What's wrong with these muthafuckas thinking they can just be getting booty in my shit?" he said, mugging Mars who walked his ass off to the pool.

I started cracking up. He looked mad for real.

"Look what you started. Why you being messy?" Dime asked me, smiling and shaking her head.

"They got me fucked up," Luca said trying to get up, but Diamond sat on that nigga and was holding him around his neck laughing.

"That shit not funny, ma. They're all in our kitchen fucking. I'm gone put Bear and Rae out. It's bad enough that we have to hear Rae screaming all night. When they ass going home son?" he said as Dime's body was shaking with laughter. That nigga was fed up. Riah and I couldn't help laughing ourselves. That's how frustrated that nigga sounded. I done started some shit.

Getting up, I went to the pool where Luna, Nya, Mars, and a few other people I didn't know were. They all were in the pool playing. Luna splashed me, so I stripped down to my swim trunks and hopped in right in front of her splashing her back. I picked her up and threw her as she was trying her best to hold on to me, laughing. Mane, this girl's smile is everything.

# 12

## LUNA

I had the best time at Nya's celebration she was back in school for the fall semester, and I knew she was gone do her shit again. I was avoiding Amod at all cost. Being around his ass made my skin crawl. I still was disgusted by the fact that he was eating some bitch's pussy in my car! I just almost threw up my brunch thinking about it. He had to go through my parents or Nya to get Lani, well mostly my parents now since the last time Nya shot his ass in the shoulder, talking bout she thought he was running up. She was lying yawl. Her petty ass did that off the strength of me. My parents were out of line taking her to the gun range faithfully after she told them about her interest in guns at thirteen. I don't know why they thought she was normal, but she wasn't.

I was at the nail shop with Alani and Jahanna. Kyrie had some business to handle, so I decided to take the girls on a date. We had done brunch before we came here and we were going to Candy Land afterwards.

"Mommy, I told this lady that this finger supposed to be purple and the rest supposed to be pink, and she made them all pink," Lani said, looking at her nails unhappy.

I told the lady to remove the pink polish from the ring fingers she was talking about and asked her to make them purple. Jahanna wanted her nails purple and lime green in a pattern. These girls were already particular about how they wanted their nails. It was so cute. I did my nails simple, deciding on a coffin shape and yellow polish.

After our nails and feet were done, we headed to Candy Land to get the girls their candy, and then I took them to the park to run around. As I sat on the bench reading *Losing Lyric* by L. Renee, I had to keep looking up since I was getting lost in the book and didn't want the girls to get snatched. Just imagine me having to explain that the girls got abducted because it was going down in a book. My parents and Kyrie will beat my ass.

After the girls tired, their selves out they were hungry and sleepy. I decided to drop them off at my parents with Nya and then head to Luca's restaurant to get take out for us. When I got in the house, Nya was on her phone sitting on the couch, and Mars was laying down with his head in her lap playing the PS4. My beautiful but pushy daughter walked right up to my face pushing at Mars' head and shoved her hands in Nya's face. Now Mars was just fine where he was for Nya to see Alani's nails. I just shook my head.

"Ohhh girl them cute, let me see yours, Jah baby," Nya said, and Jahanna did just that happily. Mars scooped Alani up.

"Why you pushing on my head and stuff Lani, why I can't be right there?" Mars said.

"You were in the way," she said with her little attitude. She gets that shit from Nya.

"No, I wasn't!" he said.

"Yeaaah."

"No."

"Yeahhh ya was!" she said again getting loud. I left them to it laughing as they were still going back and forth as I walked out the door to head to get this food.

As I drove to the restaurant, my mind just couldn't help to think about Kyrie. We had the best time on our date. I was thinking we were gone do something simple like dinner and a movie type shit, which I would have been perfectly fine with, but instead, he took me to Vegas. We had the best time gambling. I was so thirsty to give the man some pussy, but it didn't happen because my drunk ass got sick and spent the next day of our date in the hotel room bed with my stomach turning. Then Mother Nature brought her funky ass on, and I was like whyyyyy little bitch? My monthly was definitely fucking over me. I wanted Kyrie badly and was still on a high from our bomb ass date four days ago.

Pulling up at the restaurant, I parked and went inside. I headed straight to the kitchen, put in a request for my regular, and then headed to my brother's office. I don't know what I expected but certainly not the drama I walked in on. Hazel was standing at the desk going off. Luca was behind his desk standing up with Dime behind him.

"How you gone let that bitch evict me, Luca? So you mad, bitch? You're so pressed about your so-called man wanting that old thing back that you had him throw me on the streets? You're a weak ass, ugly bitch!" Hazel screamed.

*Damn, she said a mouthful!*

"Hoe pressed? Says the bum bitch who don't know that old thing is dead and washed up! Little bitch, I was nice the fuck enough. Fuck you! I don't care about you being on no streets. That's where your hoe ass belongs anyway. You definitely need a pimp, sus. Get the fuck on! Your wellbeing is not my husband's concern. Fuck is wrong with you!" Dime screamed right back.

Luca was frowning. He looked like he was going to fuck Hazel up. He pushed the hell out of her after she reached over and poked Dime on her forehead. Diamond then swung and knocked that bitch in the eye. She was trying to get around the desk, but just as security came pulling Hazel out the door, Diamond screamed, "My water broke!"

We welcomed Lula Rayari Wright into the world on September twelfth, and she was beautiful. She had Luca's dark complexion, but that's it. She was all her mama after that with her thick lips, button nose, light brown eyes, and a head full of curly hair. She was giving me baby fever. I couldn't help thinking about my love bug's born day, which was in three days.

"It was about time. Your cute little self was a week late. I was starting to think they were gone have to force you out," Nya said, holding baby Lula.

Rayna was in the room when she pushed her out, but after loving on the baby, she disappeared and so did Bear. They had been gone for a good two hours. I was getting sleepy, so I was about to go home. Nya told me she dropped the girls off at Sugar Momma's since she had to come here, and I was okay with it. Sugar Momma was the best. As I kissed my baby niece and got ready to leave, Rayna came in with Bear right behind her shaking his head. Rae's eyes were so low that you knew she was loaded. She came in with a small, gold sparkly Christmas gift box and handed it to Dime who was watching everyone hold her baby like a hawk. She wasn't playing.

"Don't nobody touch my daughter with dirty hands. There is a sink and some hand sanitizer. EVERYBODY needs to use it before touching my baby," she announced when we all rushed in to see the new addition to the family.

After opening the box Rae handed her, Diamond quickly closed it.

"RAYNA! What the fuck?" she said, shaking her head.

Luca looked inside and almost had the same reaction. He looked at Bear and said, "Nigga, why?"

Bear just shrugged and had a seat simply saying, "She specialized" and pointed to his head, making me curious about the box. They were keeping it between them though, so I dismissed it and headed out to go home. I was sleepy as hell, but I was definitely coming back to see my baby niece.

As I pulled up at my parents' house, I peeped Amod out there. Oh, look. *The nigga found HIS car.* Getting my food I picked up from Taco Bell before coming home, I got out of the car and walked right past him, but he wasn't having it.

"Luna, I'm sorry. I am. I understand if you don't want to be with me anymore. I'm fucked up for everything I did to you. I'm sorry, okay. I just want to be there for my daughter. Please allow my people and me to attend baby girl's birthday party. All I want to do is celebrate baby girl's birthday with her on her birthday."

Thinking about it, I debated back and forth for about three minutes. The sight of Amod made me sick to my stomach, but our shit had nothing to do with our daughter. Deciding to put my disgust to the side, I agreed for Amod and his family to attend the pool party that I was throwing at my parents' house.

Lani was going to Paris with my parents as a gift for them missing her birthday party due to them being in Egypt right now. Lani already talked her baby shit about it, and they agreed to make it up to her. My parents were sad as hell that Dime had the baby. They were coming back in four days, and Dime was scheduled to get induced in six days, so they thought they wouldn't miss it. They thought wrong. I knew they couldn't wait to get back to see baby Lula.

"Thank you, beautiful. I appreciate it. I could hug yo ass right now."

"Don't do that shit," I said as my entire body inwardly cringed at the thought. He had better get the fuck on.

Walking inside, I closed the door right in that nigga's face. Seeing how shit was going with Moni and Cole, I never wanted to be out here looking that dumb. Don't get it fucked up. I love Moni Lord knows I do, but her ass was looking like a clown out here with big shoes, a red nose, and the suit. My cousin was still checking for Moni though with her stupid ass.

I went upstairs to my room. I ate my food and then prepared myself to take a hot bath. These cramps had me fucked up. I was sleepy and just wanted to soak in the tub, so I did just that. When I finished in the bathroom, I threw on a big t-shirt and sweats and dove in the bed. As I was dozing off, I got a phone call. Picking it up without looking to see who it was, I answered.

"Yeahhh," I said sleepily.

"Mama!" Lani yelled in my ear, making my eyes pop open. I was so close to dreamland.

"Lani, why are you yelling?" I wanted to know.

"My bad but mom my baby cousin is here, and I want to go see her," she said, whining.

"Alani, we can go see her tomorrow. Go to sleep. Why are you not in bed?" Her ass sounded wide awake at two in the morning.

"Mommy, focus, I am in bed. Jah, Uncle Kyrie, and I are watching *The Lion King*. What time tomorrow, mommy?"

First of all that is not her uncle more like future step daddy, second Nya is banned from watching Alani. Why did she just tell me to focus like I didn't address what her little ass called me about?

"In the *morning,* Alani Nubia Wright! Go. To. Sleep, I'm gone call you. I love you, good night," I said wanting her ass off my line and low key happy that she wasn't here, or she would have been talking about meeting her little cousin all night.

"Okay, mommy, I love you too, and I'm gone be waiting," she said, and then I heard shuffling.

"I miss you, shawty. Give me kiss," Kyrie said, making the butter-flies in my stomach go crazy. *Baby, that voice.*

"I miss you too," I told him.

He is so corny with that give him a kiss shit, but I knew I wasn't no getting off the phone with him until I did, so I kissed his cheesy ass through the phone. Kissing me back, he told me good night, and he gone see me in the morning.

"Mommy, you said you were gone call me!" My eyes fluttered open to my baby big brown eyes.

Looking at the clock on the nightstand, it was nine in the morn-ing. I had a good mind to snatch her little ass under these covers, so I did just that. I held her to my chest like I'd been doing since she was a baby when we were going to sleep. She was struggling trying to get away from the cuddle I put her annoying little ass in because I told her that I was gone call her! *Why is she here?*

"She tricked me shawty, and baby Jah helped her. They are

sneaky, bruh. Why she got a key anyway?" Kyrie said, and I knew he wasn't lying. The girls were sneaky as hell and definitely knew how to put their cuteness together to get what they wanted.

Knowing first-hand how convincing the girls can be, I wasn't even mad. I sat up pulling the covers off Alani and me. She was doing the most struggling with the covers and rolled off the bed onto the plush carpet. I just watched her fall with her dramatic ass.

"I'm about to get dressed then we can go," I said, getting up and stepping over my daughter and headed right to the bathroom to get myself ready to head to the hospital so that this girl can see her baby cousin.

## 13

# LUNYA

Skype was continuously hitting me up on some let's just get together type shit, and I was so annoyed. First of all, he was still fucking Ana. That wasn't my business, but he definitely needed to take his ass somewhere. Mars and I had a long talk, and we both agreed that we were gone build up our relationship and really tried to work with one another. He told me if he was gone be with me, I had to chill with being petty. I agreed with talking out our issues if Mars promised not to fuck over me. He told me he broke up with Ana, and I was on a huge high. All we were doing was spending hella time together and having bomb ass sex. It felt good to have the nigga I was in love with.

I was in the hospital visiting my baby niece. I had Alani and baby Jah with me. It was like they became a package deal. Luna was at work, and Dime and baby Lula were getting discharged today. Alani was holding the baby and calling her Sparkly Jr. It was cute. Baby Jah didn't seem all that interested. She looked dead at Diamond and Luca and said, *"Ms. Sparkly, she cute and all that, but I don't do babies."*

Like what? You are a baby. We all couldn't do shit but laugh. She was so serious.

"It's cool, baby Jah, I respect that," Dime said, trying to be serious.

I just shook my head. I don't know how these kids got like this. Everybody wants to blame me for Alani ways but look at baby Jah.

"Rayna, you need to take this box with you," she said, holding the small, glittery cute gift box.

"Dime what? I'm about to get on a plane. You trying to get me bumped?" she said like Diamond was slow.

"Girl, get this box!" Diamond said, shaking her head laughing.

"I did this for you, and this how you do me?" Rae said, sounding heartbroken.

"Rae, you did that crazy ass shit. Now go get rid of the evidence with your irrational ass, and you just gone let her do the shit!" Dime said, looking at Bear. She sounded like Dada from *Friday After Next*. I was so tickled, and I didn't even know what the fuck was in the box.

"Mane, I can't control that violent ass midget. She hit me, and if I hit her ass back, then you gone want to fight."

"Fucking right!" Dime said with conviction.

"I don't have to deal with this I'm Rainy Rayna Rain the poet. I'm gone tell my supporters how you're doing me my listeners and poet friends. Don't play about me. I was trying to help," she said.

I truly doubted whatever that box contained she did it to "help" like she just stated, but I was over the whole thing. I had shit to do, and Luna should be off work by now. Lani's birthday party was tomorrow, and I had a list of shit to get together, so I was dropping off the girls and doing just that.

I WAS in the mall shopping for Alani. I already got hella shit for her, but I always got to go out for my child. Lani was definitely gone always be considered my firstborn. After buying some cute fits for Luna and myself, I was ready to go walking out when I saw that nigga Skype and Ana holding hands walking past me and into the mall. Making eye contact with him, I chuckled, and my phone started ringing, distracting me. I answered without looking at the name as I threw all the shopping bags in the backseat. I also had a text from Skype that I accidentally clicked on.

**Skype:** *Baby, I got to settle because your ass playing games, just be my shawty! I'd break up with Ananda if you were fucking with a nigga.*

All I could do is shake my head. *Boyyyy... and the fuck is an Ananda?* I thought as I answered my phone.

"Yeahhh?" I answered, sliding in the driver seat of my beautiful car.

"Nya, I need to talk to you."

It was Kamoni. I haven't talked to her since my celebration. She apologized and everything, but even though I had forgiven her, I still was giving her space. She sounded really messed up right now, so I went to see her. Once there, she told me some shit that fucked my head up. I didn't even know she and Zeriah were on that type of time with each other. I knew they had some shit going when we were kids, but we were kids still playing Barbie dolls and house and shit. Now that I think about it, Riah always wanted to be the daddy, and Moni wanted to be the mom while Luna and I were their twin daughters. It was starting to make sense.

Anyway, my cousin had flown back to Atlanta last month. He was gone be at Alani birthday party though. I hugged my friend. I was always gone be here for her, but she needed to catch her head though because Riah had real dreams, and best friend or not, I was at her hat if she does anything to sabotage my cousin's promising future. I told her to come to the birthday party, and she said she would think about it.

I had a few sales to make today after class, and then I was going to my parents' house to help Luna set up for the party.

~

"THIS IS SO BOMB," I said, admiring our handy work.

We had turned my parents' home into a beautiful pink and purple Egyptian themed birthday celebration. There were sparkly cups and plates, and pink and purple balloons. The silk purple and pink scarves we had gave it a bolder royal look. Alani had gifts all over this house. A gift table was in the living room, kitchen, and in the backyard, which we decorated with a Hello Kitty theme.

In the backyard was the pool party stuff. We had a slip-n-slide, the pool had hella floaties, beach balls, and water toys for all the kids that we planned to have here tomorrow. I wanted to get a bunch of water balloons, but Luna said no. I got a little cooler of water balloons anyway. Since Lani was turning five, I felt like instead of shoving her face in that beautiful Egyptian glitter frosted cake I spent good bread on, I was gone hit her ass with a couple of water balloons. It was the small ones, so she will be fine as would the rest of the kids. Luna was being too protective if you asked me. Lani wasn't too young to get hit with a water balloon. That shit doesn't even hurt.

I was tired as hell, and I started to sleep here, but I had got some calls about sales and I had two classes on Fridays, so I was gone go back to my dorm. After I made the sales, I was headed home and decided to stop at Mars' place because I missed him. He told me he was flying out of town in the morning for some business, so I was gone surprise him before he left since he was gone be gone for a few days. However, what I saw as I pulled up to his condo that he thought I didn't know about made my heart shatter in a million pieces. I watched Mars kissing Ana and smack her ass as she left out of his house. Tears rushed to my eyes, and I swear that I killed Marshad and that bitch fifty different ways in my head! Wiping my tears, I shook my head up and down and sent that *hey big head* text to Skype. I had my petty knife out — fuck Mars and that bitch Ana. I pulled off to head to my dorm.

**Skype:** *Come by me. Let me rub on that ass while we watch Friday.*
**Me:** *Okayyy.*

# 14

## MARSHAD

I had my cake and was eating it too. Why, because it was my damn cake, and of course, my ass was gone eat it. I fucked with Little tough. I even loved her ass, and I appreciated her trying to chill with the petty shit. However, on the other hand, it wasn't easy to just cut Ana off. I loved her ass too, so I kept them both. As I had this bitch Ana sucking my dick for the last time, I tried to choke her to death with my dick. This bitch was playing on me the whole time. I couldn't even be sure she ever stopped fucking with her baby dad, Skype. She was telling me her kids were with her mom and the nigga was a deadbeat. However, *he* had the fucking kids the whole time.

I stopped by the house I share with this hoe before I headed out of town, and imagine my surprise seeing this hoe kissing that man and saying bye to the kids. I sat in my car for a few sending over this bitch's information, and fifteen minutes later, I had all the information I needed. This bitch was capping. She was the fucking deadbeat.

Taking a deep breath, I went inside, and the bitch played that role great. If I didn't just see the shit, I wouldn't have known she was just loving all on her baby dad. My heart was hurting. I ain't even gone cap. This bitch really played on a nigga after I could have been left this messy ass hoe. After I came all over the bitch's face, I pushed her away from me and let her know I just wanted to see my seeds on her face one last time and to be happy with her nigga. Pulling up my pants, I went to get the shit that I had in this bitch. That nigga can take this rent payment and utilities off my hands. I had put the shit in her name, or I would have put her ass out, but I wasn't tripping on this little condo. This wasn't my primary spot anyway, so I was good regardless. Fuck this bitch.

I was pissed off. All I could do was laugh at this bitch trying to play on me. She clearly didn't know who she was fucking with. I done killed muthafuckas for less. I knew if I stayed in this bitch, I was gone kill this hoe. She's sitting here begging a nigga to stay and for what? The bitch was out of line. She was sitting here acting like she wasn't still fucking with her baby dad. I wasn't no chasing ass nigga. She was choosing who she wanted, so I was gone let her do her shit.

I was packing all my shit and getting the fuck before I killed the bitch. No pussy was worth me catching a body right now, so I was just leaving. She kept touching a nigga begging me to stay. I told the bitch to keep her hands to herself. It was over with. She could keep them fake ass tears. She wasn't crying when she was fucking and sucking her baby dad. A nigga was really trying with the bitch. Never again, I was going back to the old me— fuck relationships. A nigga just wanted to have fun and bust a nut. Fuck the dumb shit. At the end of the day, she thought she was gone play on a nigga, but better believe I ain't nobody dummy, and I don't play that shit. The bitch had better be lucky she's not dead right now, gripping on me and shit. Fuck these hoes, son.

She had to believe that I was a duck ass nigga. She was playing on my top like my career wasn't murdering muthafuckas. She wasn't worth it, plus she had kids, and although she had a nigga fucked up, I wasn't tripping. I was taking my ass to Chicago to stay with my bro and his ole lady until I felt like coming back in town. Ana's slut ass was over with. A nigga couldn't be pissed. These hoes be choosing. That's life. The bitch kept trying to touch on me and begging a nigga to fuck her. She needed to back up off me. She was never getting this dick again, I merch. If she cared about her life, she would back her friendly pussy having ass up before she be dead. That's on me.

She was crying hysterically and shit like she wasn't fucking around on a nigga. Fuck this bitch. I meant that shit. I didn't even feel fucked up about the fact that I was kicking it tough with Little. A nigga gone, she fucked up! After prying her hands off me, I grabbed all the shit I packed up and went on my way. Hopping in my green Camaro, I headed to the airport to head to Chicago. I was leaving the city. I couldn't even think about Little's sexy ass right now. I knew she was gone to feel played, but a nigga needed some space. When I get from the Chi, I would see what's good with my baby. Her ass wasn't answering my calls for shit, and to be honest, a nigga didn't even give a fuck. I knew staying here with how I was feeling was gone lead to funeral arrangements.

Pussy wasn't worth it, but a nigga couldn't stomach being disrespected. This was the second time a bitch done cheated on a nigga. There won't be a fucking third, and if there is, the bitch won't live to tell a soul about it, and that's on me.

## 15

# KYRIE

"Daddy, Uncle Kyrie's got a girlfriend, and she's my best friend Alani's mom, my cousin Moni bestie twin," baby Jah said, telling all my business to my brother.

We were at the visit, and like any other time we visited, Jahanna talked, talked, talked, and talked. I wasn't mad at it though. I knew she missed her daddy, and I knew he missed her, so I made it a point to make sure we made visits.

"Oh yeah daughter, she cute?" my brother asked like a bitch getting the tea. I shook my head.

"She's beautifulll, daddy! I want you to meet my best friend, daddy. She looks just like her. I'm gone ask Ms. Luna or Mrs. Kyrie like Uncle Ky call her if Lani could come to the next visit," she said, giggling. Baby Jah was out of line right now. I don't know where she's going since she wants to tell all a nigga business.

"Okay, tell Mrs. Kyrie I said hello, daughter," he said, smirking at me.

It was like looking in the mirror except I had locs. He had a low fade with waves all the way through. We definitely weren't no ugly ass niggas. Too bad, we didn't know where we got these good genes from since we were adopted as babies.

"Oh, I will, daddy. It's Alani birthday party today. After we leave, we are going over there. Oh and dad I'm going to Paris with her and her maw-maw and paw-paw!" she said excitedly.

He immediately raised his eyebrow at me. I started talking right away, shit no! I didn't want no smoke with this nigga behind his daughter.

"We ain't agree on that baby Jah, matter fact what I tell you?" I said, looking at her.

"To ask my daddy, well daddy, can I go?" she said in her cute, small voice and giving Kyren them big pretty eyes, looking just like that damn Jahresa.

Baby Jah is like a reincarnation of that girl. I don't know how this nigga is gone tell her no. I know my brother. He trusted me to make decisions with Jahanna, including who I allowed her to be with and around, but he didn't like outsiders on no level, especially when it came to baby girl. I've been fucking with Claya for years, and she hasn't even been able to meet baby Jah.

"Daughter, see if they will be willing to come visit so that I can meet them, and then I'll decide if you can go."

She seemed content with that answer as she colored a picture for her dad, leaving me to joke with my brother.

"Mrs. Kyrie, huh?" he said.

"Yeah, little bitch, Mrs. Kyrie," I responded.

"Okay, be cool. I ain't mad, big bro. You seem happy. Thank you, my nigga" He always felt the need to thank me each visit for taking baby Jah in. He didn't have to though. I know the definition of a godfather, and I didn't accept the position because it sounded good.

"You know I got you always, bro. How are you holding up?"

"I'm straight as long as she's good," he said, looking at baby Jah. He was a good father, and I know it fucked him up to have to raise her from jail.

We talked for a little more before the visit was ending. Baby Jah was about to hand him the color sheet, but she forgot to put by baby Jah, so she moved it back, wrote it, and then handed it to him.

"This goes hard, baby girl. Why is the elephant black though, daughter?" he asked her. Hell, I wanted to know too because she knew they were gray.

She giggled and said, "Black is beautiful, daddy. That's why I'll see you next visit. I love you, daddy. Keep your head up. Oh, and daddy chin up. We are giants." She hugged him tightly.

"Yes, indeed to both, baby girl."

I could tell he was touched. I felt that shit and not just because he was my twin. Looking at him, you can see her leaving tore him up. I knew it killed him to have to part ways with his daughter each visit. I dapped him up, and baby Jah and I left out to head to the birthday party. I missed my brother. I was gone do everything I could to see about reopening his case. Believe that!

LUNA WAS RUNNING around this bitch annoyed but trying to hold it together for baby girl. I didn't know what was up, but she was slamming shit, talking shit, and she was ready to flash on her sister about some damn water balloons. I couldn't let my shawty's day go like this. The girls were happy and oblivious, but I didn't want that energy to rain on their parade. I was thinking of a way to brighten her day as she made the candy bags. Her baby dad was here too, and I was sure that could be another reason why she was so pissed. Nya did have a bit of an attitude, but she seemed to be holding it together better than Luna as she chased the kids around spraying them with a big ass water gun. Everybody seemed to be having a good time for the most part but Luna, so I had to get my lady together.

Some pretty light skin woman came in and asked about some more juice, and shawty said, "Fuck that juice. I don't have no more shit!"

"Awe, okayyyyyy," she said with wide eyes and got the fuck on. *Yeah, let me get her together.*

"Say, take your ass upstairs. You cutting up. These people didn't do anything to you."

"I got to get these—"

"Man, take your ass upstairs!"

She was mumbling some shit, but I didn't give a fuck as long as she took her ass upstairs. She was taking her frustration out on people who ain't did shit to her, and it wasn't cool at all. I got the extra juice to bring out to the kids, finished the candy bags, and told Nya to hold it down for a few minutes for me. When I went upstairs, Luna was pulling shit out her closet. I was confused as fuck. I never saw her act like this before, but I was sure gone figure this shit out with her.

"What's up with you, shawty?" I said, sitting on the bed.

"This closet is a mess."

"Mane, come here. What's wrong?"

"Nothing," she said, getting up and trying to walk past me. I grabbed her. Just staring at her, she broke down.

"I'm just tired of this shit. I wouldn't change having Alani for nothing in this world, but I just wish I wasn't stuck dealing with Amod and his stupid ass family," she said with tears sliding down her cheeks, making my heart hurt. *Damn, I was feeling this girl.* I wiped her tears.

"Shawty, it's baby girl's day. You don't need to be focused on them people. It's cool give them today. Fuck that nigga and enjoy Alani's birthday. Stop letting them muthafuckas get a reaction out of you. Baby, fuck them! Real shit."

"You don't understand. They're always saying negative shit like I'm not a damn good mother and person. All they do is bring negativity. I knew I should have never agreed for them to be here today, I'm not perfect, but I'm a damn good mom," she said crying harder she was working herself up, I didn't understand why she felt the need to get validation from them, so I asked her ass that.

"It's not validation. It's just all that negative shit weighs me down."

"Fuck them! If they're negative, then remove yourself. You're up here crying being rude to your daughter's guests, and for what, shawty?"

"I'm just frustrated, Kyrie," she said, trying to get up. I was gone help with that frustration, real shit, but right now was about baby girl. I had something for Luna later. I pulled her back and laid her on the bed, and I rolled on top of her.

"Shawty, you need to pull it together. I promise I'm gone take care of you when everybody leaves. Do you need your pussy ate so that you can get through the rest of the day until I can handle that frustration?"

"I meannnnn," she said, and I tongued kissed her as I slipped my hand in her jeans playing with her pussy.

## 16

# LUNA

I swear it was a pool between my thighs as Kyrie played in my pussy. It's been a minute since I had some, so I wanted to get through this party and then be blessed by my man. We weren't official yet. He had some little bitch he was fucking with tough, and she was on my nigga hard. She called his shit at least six times a day since he stopped fucking with her, so I'm saying, I know the dick pressure. I bit my lip and spread my legs, allowing Ky full access to my coochie. He was sucking on my neck, and I couldn't help the wetness going on at this moment. He pulled my jeans and panties off and slid down my body, licking up and down my slit. I was gripping the sheets tightly as I bit my lip trying to be as quiet as I can, but Kyrie wasn't having that shit. He wanted to hear me, so he was going dumb slurping and licking on my pussy. I was so ready that I started cumming, and I felt all the frustration from Amod's bitch ass and his annoying ass family leaving my body.

After Ky made me cum two more times, he came up. I wanted to go to sleep, but I had to pull it together like my nigga said for my daughter. As I was breathing heavily from that fire ass head he blessed me with, he slapped my thigh, making my eyes pop open.

"That pussy is good as fuck, shawty. Come on. Get your ass up."

I dragged myself out the bed, went in the bathroom to wash my kitty, changed into a champagne color dress that was off the shoulder pulled on clean pair of panties, and slid into my white furry slides. My hair was in a ponytail at my nape, and I had a deep side part with a swoop. I felt refreshed.

Heading downstairs, I had to find Trendy. I didn't mean to take my annoyance out on her. She was inside serving the girls the white strawberry cranberry juice in the cute plastic champagne glasses. My baby was sitting on her little throne with her hair up in a plait twisted updo with gold clips and a light champagne-colored dress that had a crisscross back. The dress went past her ankles. Her crown was positioned on her head, and she had gold, sparkly polish on her nails and little hoops in her ears. She was too cute, and I couldn't stop looking at her pretty self. *Damn, I really made her little ass!*

Trendy's badass son Emperor was running in and out. He would stare at Alani for a few then leave out to the backyard. He did this three times in my presence before his daddy August finally told his little ass something.

Jahanna was looking just as cute in a white dress with gold glitter. She also had a tiara on her head. Alani wasn't for none of that. It was a must that her best friend had a tiara and pretty dress like her, and she was so serious when baby Jah came in here in plain clothes she said, "Oh no friend where is your dress?"

Baby Jah responded, "In the car shawty, chilllll!" Like these little girls gave me so much life. I was so in love with their little bond and personalities.

After Trendy served the little queens and the other little girls their pizza and Jell-O cups, she went into the kitchen. I followed her. I needed to apologize to my girl. I took my frustration out on her that was wrong of me.

"Say Trend, my bad for snapping at you."

"You good, my girl. Ky already came to me telling me you were frustrated. He got you together because you were on that level. *"Fuck that muthafucking juice!"* I was like well damn, fuck that juice. These kids better drink water," she said, laughing, causing me to laugh.

"Gurllll, I apologize I was out of line," I told her sincerely.

"You're good. I know how shit be. Honestly, birthday parties are the worse. I see that duck ass nigga Amod in here, and I peeped his mom was on bullshit, so I knew you were just having a moment. Boo, you good, honestly."

"Awe, thanks for understanding, I apprec—"

"Mama, I'm ready to change. We're about to go to the pool."

"Come on, Queen Alani."

I went upstairs with my love bug and baby Jah following behind me. The other little girls who were at the Egyptian royal event were changing downstairs. I grabbed the shopping bag with the girls' new swimming suits and helped them both out of their dresses Alani had a pink swimming suit with Hello Kitty on it, and baby Jah had a purple swimming suit with Princess Tiana and a green frog on it. I took Alani hair out of the updo allowing the plaits to fall loosely past her shoulders. Since baby Jah hair was in a neat bun, I took it out and put two French braids in her hair. Washing their hair was going to be a process.

They put their furry slides on. Alani has purple ones, and Jah had lime green ones. They both grabbed their towels that match their swimsuits. Amod hired a clown to make balloon animals, and his effort was appreciated, but he clearly doesn't know his daughter— Lani hated clowns. Hell, baby Jah too, she took off as soon as she saw the damn clown and came back with Kyrie

"Uncle Ky, get *IT* out of here," she said on the verge of tears. I know you fucking lying. He let this baby watch *IT*?

We made the clown leave, and Mod was upset and left, but I didn't give a fuck. He needed to take is ugly ass mom and his creepy ass uncle with him. Between the three of them, that's why I was in such a sour ass mood Amod thought shit was sweet until he saw Kyrie, and he's just been on his bullshit ever since.

Nya came and sprayed Lani and Jah with the water gun. They took off running and went to the slip-n-slide. The water balloons weren't all that bad like I thought. Only one kid was crying, and that was little Emperor because baby Jah hit him in the face with a water balloon. After he hit Alani with three back-to-back, baby Jah wasn't sorry, and she let Trendy and August know it too. All Kyrie could do is shake his head. August told Emperor to shake it off, and he did, but he stayed away from baby Jah for the rest of the party. These damn kids were a mess! That was new school shit.

Zeriah had come through, and he had hella gifts. Rayna and Bear had already gone back to Atlanta, but they celebrated with Alani prior to leaving. Dime and Luca were here as well. Diamond was not a friendly new mom at all. She wasn't for none. No little kids other than Alani could touch my baby niece. She was telling kids all day to give them fifty feet! "Get back!" She had to say that at least a hundred times. She's a mess.

After cake, ice cream, and a successful party, I passed out candy bags and kicked all those babies out so that the cleanup crew could get my parents' home back right. Even Alani and baby Jah had to go. They went with Nya to Dime and Luca's place. I was beyond ready for mommy time after a successful birthday party for my baby girl.

Releasing the ponytail, I walked into my bedroom and was in awe at the roses and candles that were in the room. Ky was sitting on the bed shirtless showing off his tattoos. I was drooling— daddy was so fineeeee! Walking up to me, he kissed me, peeled me out of my dress, and led me to the bathroom where there were more candles and soft music playing. The tub was filled with bubbles. He kissed my cheek and led me into the tub. I felt sexy I was ready to bust it open for Ky right now, but he had put a lot of thought into this. He put a purple silk robe on the hook of the bathroom door and left out, leaving me alone. I washed up and soaked relaxing.

I couldn't waitttttt to have sex with Kyrie. He'd been making love to my mind and spirit since I met him, and I couldn't be happier right now to give him my body. After I washed up and rinsed off, I stepped out, dried off, and put the silk robe on. Fuck this robe though. Entering my bedroom, there were chocolate covered strawberries, and Ky was waiting for me. I just wanted to jump on his fine ass, but I went at his pace. He took the robe off me and laid me on my stomach. Using body oil, he rubbed me down. He paid extra attention to my booty. As he rubbed the oil all over my skin, he flipped me over onto my back and rubbed oil all over my titties.

*NIGGA, COME ON!* My entire body was screaming for him to do some freaky shit. My pussy was ready for him. My heart too, hell boffumm! I was falling in love, and I didn't want to stop it. I embraced it. As he ate my pussy again, I cried out and begged him to put the tip in. He had a beautiful dick, and I wish I could draw because I'll spend a lot of my time sketching that muthafucka. I licked my lips, and before I could say anything, my breath got caught in my throat as he pushed at my entrance.

"I'm proud of you, shawty. You pulled through," he said as he entered me, making my pussy wetter. Tears instantly rushed to my eyes at how good the dick felt. *Yup, I'm in love!*

### Three Months Later

I have been going strong with Ky for close to four months. We were so in love. The girls were damn near sisters. Lani was going to prison visits with Kyrie and Jah faithfully, and my parents even agreed to meet Kyren so that Jah could go to Paris with them next month. Christmas was approaching, and I was looking forward to the holidays like always.

Today Alani and baby Jah was helping me make cupcakes. Well not really, it was more like Lani was demanding shit and eating the frosting and baby Jah already told me she was fake helping to lick the bowl and spoon. I had been preparing for the annual Christmas party we have every year at my parents, and they were in the way. Kyrie was out handling business, so I immediately dismissed the thought of him coming to get the girls. My parents were out Christmas shopping, and it was finals week for Nya before she went on break.

There was a knock at the door, and it was Amod.

"What you doing here?"

"I told you I was taking Alani to a birthday party for my girl's daughter." *Damn, I forgot.*

"Hold on." I closed the door in his face. I still don't like his ass!

"Alani, why you ain't say nothing about the birthday party your daddy was taking you to today?"

"I forgot, mama," she said dryly.

"Welllll?"

"Can Jah come?"

"Ask your daddy," I told her, going back to making the cake.

She left out and came back. "He said yeah, mom."

I called Ky to see if it was cool, but he didn't answer. Calling him three more times, I didn't get an answer, so I allowed baby Jah to go. After the girls left, I was able to get a lot more done for this Christmas party.

# 17

## LUNYA

I was done playing this back and forth game with Mars. We had been spending so much time together that I forgot all about Ana I saw her leaving his condo. All I could imagine is her fucking and sucking on my man. I know he wasn't just holding hands with that hoe. Heartbroken was an understatement. I was so over the bullshit. I didn't understand why Mars couldn't just get it right with me. I know I'm petty as hell, but if he just acted like a good nigga and stopped trying to play games with me, we wouldn't even be in this situation now or back when I was younger.

I love the hell out of Mars, but he had me feeling like he wanted me to choose me or him, which was fucked up. I choose me, and when I do he acts like he lost his damn mind He's been blowing my phone up since the night I witnessed Ana coming out his condo. When I saw them together, it felt like shot to my chest. Of course, Mars held the gun! I wanted him to know that I was over all the bull-shit, so he was one more phone call away from being blocked. Add that to the fact that I ain't seen Mars' ass in months since he took that "business trip" the same one he supposedly was taking when I wanted to surprise his ass and caught Ana leaving. I swear he's just bullshit!

Honestly, I been kicking it with Skype out of spite and would be lying if I said I wasn't developing feelings for him. He didn't press me too hard about fucking because no lie, I wasn't ready! He cut Ana's hoe ass off. That bitch stayed trying to use their kids as an excuse. It seemed like she was blowing his shit up every time I was around.

Gathering my book sack, I had to make another sale before I had to head to class it was right at the end of the first semester. Matter fact today was the last day for me to take the final for my five courses. Knowing I couldn't be late for my final, I went to class bringing the weed with me to make the sale afterwards. I knew I killed the first four exams. I had one more left to go, and I was hyped to get finished. Some commotion broke out, and the police came into my classroom with K9s, and my heart sped up. I had about seven grams of weed on me right now, and I am scared as fuck.

"I'm Officer Bruce, and we are going to be doing a thorough check of each person and their dorms before we leave today."

*Oh, shit! Fuck think, think!* I was trying to think of anything to get out of this situation, but as the dogs went crazy and Officer Bruce came up to me, he immediately called the female cop who was with them to search me. She discovered the seven grams in the secret pocket inside of my jean jacket. *FUCK! MY MOM'S GONE KILL ME!*

When they searched my dorm, they found a half a pound, and I went to jail for possession. I was scared to call my parents or my brother, so I called Skype. He wanted my cookie so bad, but I was not fucking Skype. He can eat my pussy all day long, and I even blessed him with some bomb ass head, but no matter how bad I tried, I could not bring myself to fuck this man. Although he was pressed, he respected my wishes. Anyway, the day I got bumped on possession I was too scared to call my parents and knew if I called Luca, he would call my parents, so I called Skype instead.

I'VE BEEN DUCKED off in his townhouse with him and Ana's kids for two weeks. My parents and siblings had been calling, but I just couldn't bring myself to go home yet, but then again, I was over the constant begging for pussy that Skype was doing lately. The shit was turning me off! Then, I told that nigga I was waiting for marriage, and he proposed to me two days ago! Now, I didn't agree to the marriage, but the beautiful ass sapphire princess cut diamond with broken shards of baby pink diamonds around the band was definitely on my finger! In consideration of this bomb ass ring, I told Skype that we were moving too fast, but I was in love with him— lie. I had love for him, but the only nigga I was *in* love with had me fucked up, and I haven't seen him in fucking months!

The phone calls that I refused to answer stop coming about a week ago, and I'll be lying if I said I wasn't feeling a way about the shit! Really nigga? You messed over me! How are you gone stop blowing MY shit up? At the end of the day, no matter how much I love Marshad, I wouldn't allow him to make me feel like I wasn't worth having, especially when this nigga Skype just bought this bomb ass ring.

Today the kids were going to their grandmother's, and I was grateful because their constant arguing and breaking shit had my head hurting. Skype had gone to drop them off, so it was just me at the house. I was drifting off when there was a knock at the door. Trying to ignore it because this is not my house, I closed my eyes tightly. However, the person was so persistent that I decided just to take a message just in case it was important. Opening the door dressed in one of Skype's hoodies and boy shorts, I went to open the door.

"Damn, you just love my sloppy seconds, toddler ass bitch."

"May I take a message?" I said dismissively and rubbed my eye blinding that bitch with my ring. *Hoe, stop playing with me.*

This bitch was too angry about my pretty ass engagement ring that she swung on me, and we went blow for blow fighting. I was beating that ass, but she also got some good hits up off me. I felt my eye swelling up when she got a decent ass hit in, but I was still fucking her up. She hit me in the mouth, pissing me clean the fuck off when I tasted blood in my mouth. I beat that bitch's face making sure the sharpness of all these fucking carats on my ring peeled her skin. I don't know when Skype got here, but the next thing I know, he is pulling me off that bitch.

"HOW COULD YOU SKYLOU! How could you do ME Like this? Nigga ME, the mother of your children. I've sacrificed everything to be with YOU! How could YOU?" she screamed, breaking down.

I didn't care I had no sympathy for her ass if anything the bitch should have fallen back from my nigga when I told her to, and we wouldn't be here! It's her fault.

"Yes, little bitch, he did, and you're invited to the wedding *tonight* along with my step kids!" I told her all the way on my petty bullshit, and as far as I was concerned, I will be Mrs. SKYLOU PARKER tonight!

OKAY, so I didn't think this shit through. I did marry Skype, not that night, but a week after. The issue is Skype wanted sex from his wife. We'd been married for a week, and he was pressing me hard for the pussy. I done used every excuse that I could think of to hold him off starting with me being on my period ending with I wanted it to be special because we had a courthouse wedding. The nigga then booked a resort to Berlin, and we were set to leave out in three days.

This shit is spiraling out of control. I need to take my ass home! The only person I been in contact with was Luna, who was covering for me, and Ivory, who was trying to get me down to Chicago. Now with school fucked up and the shit that I got myself into with Skype, I was seriously considering taking my ass to Chicago to regroup. I realize my ass might have gone a smidget too far being petty trying to get some get back. I received a call from Ivory as I packed all my bags.

"Hello?"

"Nya, so you're coming for sure, right? Brasi is looking forward to seeing you again."

"Ivoryyyy, I'm a married woman. Don't get me caught up in no mess with Brasi's fine chocolate ass!"

"You are grown. Can't nobody get you in no mess but you. I'm just passing on the message. If you don't want to get in no mess, keep your legs closed!"

"Gurlllll!"

"Gurl nothing, I got your ticket already. I'm going to send the information to your phone, aiight."

"Okay thank you so much, Ivory. I really appreciate you!"

"Always you know I got your back, Nya baby."

"I'll see you soon."

"Yup you will and keep your legs closed while you're here, bitch."

"Byee." I clicked on her ass.

Brasi is Sway's right hand man, and like I said before, he was a fine chocolate ass man. When Sway used to come visit Ivory when we were dorm mates, he will bring Brasi. If there was ever a man that had me convinced that I could ever get over Marshad, it was him.

I didn't know what the fuck I was about to do about Skype, but I felt like a dumb bitch at the moment. I haven't been on a love connection/ attraction kick with Skype since I was sixteen I'll be twenty in two weeks. I had the right mind to call that bitch Ana and give her this fucking ring. I didn't want to be married, but I know my stupid ass should have thought about that *before* the paperwork. The fucked up part is as we were leaving the courthouse, I ran into Sasha, a stylist at my mother shop, and as I conversed with her, Skype wasted no time telling her I was his wife, so much for keeping this marriage on the hush. I already know she told my mother.

Packing all of my bags, I loaded my bags into my Lexus and drove home to my parents. When I entered the house, all eyes went to me. The room was so thick. I didn't know what the fuck was going on, and I had no chance to figure it out before my mother slapped the taste out my mouth making me instantly start crying because there was no way I could fight my mama. Luckily, my daddy got her away from me, but the glare he pinned me with hurt worse than my stinging cheek. With blurry eyes, hurt feelings, and a shattered heart, I left the house and headed straight to the airport. Fuck it, Chicago here I come.

# 18

# DIAMOND

This shit was ridiculous my daughter is three months old, and I'm supposed to be learning how to be a new mother and planning a wedding, but the drama twins done stole the muthafucking show on me being happy in love with my man and baby girl. Luca doesn't play any games about his sisters, so imagine him getting a call from Mrs. Nubia that Lunya been missing for weeks, got bumped on a possession charge, *and* got married, not to mention when we came in this bitch, Kyrie was choking the fuck out of Luna causing Luca to shoot his ass.

We didn't know what the fuck was going on, but we surely needed somebody, anybody, hell everybody, to make it make sense and right when Luna was about to explain as she cried her eyes out with Kyrie's blood on her, in walked the runaway girl. Babyyyy I'm sure Nya couldn't have seen the distress and heartbreak her twin had going on or even Kyrie bleeding on the floor because Mrs. Nubia Wright was on her bullshit! She was about to fuck Lunya up, and after a pimp slap that had *me* wondering if I needed to have Mrs. Nubia money on time, Mr. Wright snatched up his wife and pinned Nya with the coldest look ever that had her crying harder than the slap her mother just delivered before she ran out of the door.

Now I am no stranger to drama with a hot-headed best friend like Rayna, but this was some new level shit. I was so lost that somebody needed to find me NEOWW, not to mention I had my own shit to be worried about. After the birth of Lula, it was safe to say that Hazel would no longer be an issue considering Rayna's unstable ass gifted me the bitch's finger! She really needed to stop watching *Paid In Full,* and I told Bear's ass that and THIS is WHY! She's getting fucked up ideas anytime Rae watches a movie more than three times in a week timeframe! I don't know if they killed Hazel or not. I'm sure that Rayna would gladly tell yawl herself. I didn't want to know. I am NOT an accomplice.

Remember diamonds are forever, and nobody really wants to lose a diamond, so my ex's been trying to get me back, and I've been ignoring his ass, but he popped up in Louisiana, and I knew I needed to tell Luca before it started looking like I'm on some shady shit. Amir needed to leave me the hell alone. I just wanted to plan my wedding and raise my daughter, but that's another story for another day.

# 19

## KYRIE

It was visiting day with Kyren, and baby Jah didn't want to go— red flag! I asked her why, but she didn't want to tell me and started crying. My heart wasn't feeling right. My niece was acting strange, and I didn't know why. I needed to know what was going on because I had to explain shit to my brother why his daughter didn't want to visit or why she wanted Alani to come over instead of going over there for the last seven days. I asked Luna about it, and she was just as confused. She tried to talk to baby Jah about it, but she refused to talk to her. She just kept crying every time we asked her if she and Alani got into it or something, but Jahanna said no, so we were lost as fuck now.

Baby girl doesn't want to see her dad when she usually can't wait to see my brother, so it was very strange. Now, I never want to force Jah to go to the jail if she doesn't want to, but at the same time, I couldn't get through to her, which was a terrifying feeling. I needed my baby to be acting like herself, and she wasn't. I made the decision to bring her to visit anyway. If I couldn't get through to her, I knew Kyren could. When he called last night, she didn't want to talk. Even though I knew this was gone worry my brother and make him uneasy, I had to tell him how strange she'd been acting. We had missed a couple of visits due to my business getting in the way, but it was extremely vital that baby girl saw her father today. I requested a private room. With the way my heart was feeling, it had to be some heavy shit for baby Jah not to want to speak on it.

"Daddy, I don't want you to be mad at me, Uncle Kyrie, or Lani. I'm sorry."

Jahanna was crying so hard that I couldn't help the tears that came to my eyes. Add in the fact that Kyren looked like he wanted to murder some shit, and there was nothing good about this situation. Jahanna didn't want me in the room when she talked to her dad about whatever was bothering her, and no cap, that hurt a nigga's feelings, but I was more concerned about what had her in tears like this. When she finally revealed it, I got sick to my stomach, and I felt like I failed my niece.

"I think it's a better idea to have Sugar Momma looking after baby Jah for now. They reopened my case, and I don't know if I can trust your ass with the most important person in my life. This is my sanity right here, and either you made a bad judgment call, or you're not paying the fuck attention, but *both* are unacceptable when it comes to my fucking daughter, NIGGA!" he gritted, but he was sure to be quiet not to wake baby Jah up. She had cried herself to sleep.

I knew I had no right to disagree with this nigga. Regardless if I would give my life for baby Jah or not, the fact that she was sexually abused was on me, and I was gone kill that bitch Luna for putting my niece in danger and having my brother questioning me as if I couldn't be trusted with his daughter.

As I watched Sugar Momma come in and pick up baby Jah, I wanted to cry like a bitch, not only because she was being taken from me, which hurt like fuck, but because she went through something that every man fears when they have little girls, and I felt responsible. As I sped through traffic, the only thought that kept playing in my head is how the fuck did she let this shit happen.

## 20

# LUNA

Hold the fuck up! Why did my baby just start acting differently when this nigga came into the room? If I don't do shit else, I pay attention to my child. If Alani Nubia Wright breaths differently, I peep it. My daughter was not acting like she needed to. She was just being her usual self until dude walked his ugly ass in here. I recall him saying she was looking "grown" in her pink Hello Kitty one-piece swimsuit at her birthday party. That shit rubbed me wrong. Now my daughter is acting weird around this nigga! My heartbeat increased as I called Lani over to me.

"Come here, love bug." She looked at him hesitating, making my pressure rise.

As she walked towards me, the fact that she kept looking at this man had me ready to call Luca. The way my kid acting right now is scaring the hell out of me. This is her father's uncle. Did I put my baby at risk by dismissing his weird ass comments? What did he do to my daughter? Was the one-piece Hello Kitty swimsuit too "grown"? Were her four-year-old curves so enticing that this man will be looking at my baby like a grown ass woman?

Tears rushed to my eyes as he looked at me. I will kill this man right here right now. My whole body was shaking, and I am about to fucking lose it! Before I could do anything, my mother grabbed Alani and brought her upstairs. Rage consumed my body. I wanted this man dead! I even wanted Amod dead. I told him countless times that his uncle was a creep.

"I didn't do shit to that little grown bitch. She's lying on me " he spat, and I instantly I busted that nasty sick nigga in the face with the heavy candle on my parents' end table as tears rushed down my face.

I was shattered. I couldn't believe that this grown man did something to my innocent ass daughter. I was breaking down as my father rushed and got rid of that child molesting ass nigga. I didn't know exactly what the hell he did, but I knew the signs, and I was sick to my fucking stomach. I was crying so hard, and the blood leaking from the gash in my hand, or the long piece of glass stuck in it didn't come close the agony I was feeling over...

"BITCH, YOU PUT MY NEICE AT RISK!" A pissed off Kyrie came storming in. He came right up to me and wrapped his hands around my throat. I placed my hands on his dripping my blood all over him as tears slid from my eyes. I was embracing my life slipping away until my brother stormed in punching Kyrie and shot him in his chest.

"LUCAAAA, NOOOOOO!" I screamed with my heart shattering into pieces.


To Be Continued

# COMING SOON

## PRESSED BY LOVE: SHOT CLOCK

**Zeriah "Riah" Lewis**

I stood off to the side next to my brother and his shawty Rayna. My attention was on my little cousin's best friend. Say, I'd been trying to get Kamoni's fine ass to be my yeah again for a minute. She was fine as fuck with light brown skin, curly hair, big titties, and a round ass. She had pouty lips, and she was too fucking fine to be sweating that bum ass nigga Cole. Since the age of twelve, Kamoni has been my little secret, my favorite one at that. I don't come to this bitch often. I am not a fan of Louisiana and being that I left so young, it didn't feel like home to a nigga.

It was my older cousin's Luca and his girl Diamond's baby shower, and since he's been training me for my upcoming season, I was thugging it in New Orleans until I got ready to take my ass back home, which is Atlanta Georgia. When Lunya ducked off outside, I walked up to Moni. She was looking sexy as shit in a red two-piece skirt and halter top showing off that body. Her hair was pulled up, and she had a few of her natural curls framing her face. The letter Z with a basketball heart attached to it at the nape of her neck had me reminiscing to the day she got it when she was fifteen. Kamoni Amora Lewis is what she called herself back then, and hell, I miss the way she used to get all giddy by my presence.

"Zeriah, get away from me," she said with a salty ass attitude.

I didn't too much give a fuck about it. No matter how far the distance or her fucked up attitude, she will always be my baby.

"You'd rather chase bum ass niggas, huh? That what's you like now, shawty?" I pressed up on her a little bit, nothing major to draw anyone's attention, but just enough for her to feel me. I was laid back, and my temper was almost nonexistent. All I really give a fuck about is basketball, my family, and this ditzy ass girl in front of me

"I've been doing the shit since I was fifteen, so why not keep it going?" she said sarcastically.

I chuckled. She can have that one. She was still pissed, and I get it, yet she shouldn't play games that she's not fucking ready for. I'm a ballplayer, a spectacular defense player to be more specific. The game that Kamoni wanted to play, she would lose. She always loses.

"That was real cute, shawty. Continue chasing lames and bums, baby girl, we both know I am neither. You still mad? You miss this dick, huh?" I said as she tried to turn away, causing me to snatch her close to my chest as I whispered in her ear while tracing the tattoo with my tongue that I paid for when I was sixteen.

"Let. Me. Go. Zeriah," she said with a shaky voice. She was pissed, and I smirked as I released her.

I made eye contact with that lame ass nigga Cole. I grinned wider. That nigga is bitch made, and I didn't give a fuck what nobody said. He worked side by side with Mars, his right hand man. They got hired on with my cousin and brother around the same time. I never fuck with Cole, and I'm man enough to admit it had a lot to do with the way he treated the girl who had my heart. Niggas want my shawty and don't even know how to treat my bitch properly. Moni's been looking unfamiliar with her actions when it comes to this nigga. I wasn't with the shit. I was falling back slightly, giving her time to do better because regardless of our history and the shit that went down between us, she knew better. I would never disrespect her the way she allowed this nigga to. That's her shit though. She's gone always be mine, and if nobody else knew what the fuck it was, she did.

I let her walk off like she was mad at the world, knowing that she was really pissed because I had that pussy wet. I drifted back over to my brother. He had Rae on his lap and wouldn't let her up. I have never seen my bro so possessive over a bitch, I told my brother just that, yet that Rayna was with the shit

"That's queen bitch, bitch!" she snapped at my ass when I let that shit slip about how caught up my big bro is. He didn't even check her smart mouth ass for talking to his little bro like that. *Pressed ass nigga.*

"Bear, damn, I can't go pee?"

"Nah, yo midget ass might get snatched the fuck up again."

"In a house full of your people? Nigga, let me go for I bat yo ass."

"Bat? Where did you learn that word from, baby? Yo proper ass don't even sound right."

"Just because I don't sound all country, I don't sound right?"

"Country?" I said at the same time as Bear. She got us fucked up. We are from the city you heard me. Fuck is she talking about country.

"Yes, country, now say baby," she smirked. My brother just ignored her and pulled her up. Slapping her ass, he finally let her go handle her business. He watched her disappear up the stairs and started talking to me.

"Don't start no shit with that nigga Cole while you here for the summer. Let that shit go and focus on what the fuck you here for."

"Man, get the fuck out of here I'm good. Fuck that nigga, and I stay focus. My eye is on the target," I told my brother.

Bear has been like a father to me as well, but that nigga knew he wasn't my daddy. As long as he remembered that our father was dead and he is my older brother, I was Gucci. I hated when he crossed that line though. I was only five going on six when our father died, and Bear was thirteen. We are seven years apart. I'll be twenty-one next month, and he will be twenty-seven in September. My older brother taught me all that I know about grinding, education, and the importance of character. I wanted to be just like him. Where he had a gift in drawing that he turned into a tattoo franchise, I was gifted at winning games and definitely on my way to the NBA. There is no I in team, yet there are three in Zeriah Brian Lewis. Anybody who knows me knows I was the fucking team at Morehouse University. I am still a team player. I'm just confident that muthafuckas weren't seeing the rank we had without me, and that's just a fact, look up my stat. I'm not capping.

Besides being a beast on the court, I was good with numbers. I helped my brother and cousin manager their books when their business started flourishing. I am far from a dumb nigga. Hell, I'm not a thug, gangsta, hitman or none of that shit. I'm just a confident hooping nigga with a bright future ahead of him. I can beat some ass too. The boxing classes I took as a hobby every summer since I was four up until seventeen should have my hands registered as weapons. Ball is my life, and boxing is just something I enjoyed for so long. It's prepared me for hard practices as well as keeps me in shape.

I had tattoos all over my body due to being Zyair's experimental project growing up. Becoming addicted to tattoos, I lucked up having a tattoo artist as a brother. I had snuck and got my first tattoo at twelve, and it was an ugly ass basketball that Bear had to cover up. He wouldn't let me get any more until I turned fourteen.

"All I know nigga is that I'm not mixing in your shit. Don't make me shoot your hard headed ass!" *He will do it.* I don't give a fuck. No man put fear in my heart, not even my disrespectful older brother.

"Yeah, whatever," I said, walking off into the kitchen.

My Auntie Nubia, which is my father NuZy's twin sister, was slamming shit, cursing aloud. She was big mad. I already knew my younger cousin Nya was the cause. She stayed pissing my auntie off.

"Think she gone be getting drinks and shit in my house? Oh no, that little spoiled ass girl got me twisted. She gone make me bust her—"

"Whoa, you good, Auntie? You want smoke," I said, laughing

"Nephew, you not gone have a cousin soon! I brought her in this world, and I'll take her ass out. She got me twisted," she said, storming out the kitchen with her long locs flowing behind her.

I grabbed a drink and headed back into the living room, the party was dying down, and I was ready to get the fuck. My brother and Rae were catching a flight early in the morning to head back to Atlanta, and although I wanted to be right with them my cousin, Luca was the best coach I ever had since I was a youngin'. He was taught by the best, and he could have gone pro if he didn't let it go. Luca would tell me every time that it just wasn't his calling. He loved the game, and my father was hard on him. However, after my father died, he didn't have the heart for it. My father, NuZy Brandon Lewis, was no joke. He was huge on defense, and it showed in the way Luca trained me, which is why I'm the warden. Get past me if you can, but it won't be easy, and nine times out of ten, they were passing the ball. They knew I wasn't for no bullshit once I hit that court.

I dapped my brother up and told my cousin I was heading back to his crib to get some rest. We had training in the morning. As I walked outside to my gray Charger, I saw Moni crying and going back and forth with that lame ass nigga Cole. Shaking my head, I just kept it pushing hoped in my whip and headed to my cousin fire ass mansion.

.

CPSIA information can be obtained
at www.ICGtesting.com
Printed in the USA
LVHW021021040819
626317LV00005B/206/P